COLLECTION FOLIO

REISER

ViVE LES FEMMES!

Albin Michel

À MARIE - FRANÇOISE

PAPA SALAUD

11

13

PHILOSOPHIE À LA PETITE SEMAINE

ZINCS EN OR

LES RÈGLES DU DÉTOURNEMENT

21

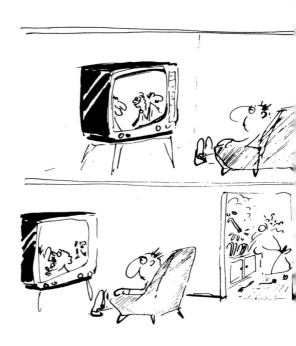

LA PETITE NIÈCE DU ROI DE L'ÉTAIN ENLEVÉE EN SUISSE... LA PETITE NIÈCE DU ROI DU PLOMB N'EN MÈNE PAS LARGE!...

31

32

CONCOMBRE

35

ÇA SERAIT LE TEST.
S'IL LE FAIT, C'EST QU'IL EST VRAIMENT AMOUREUX, S'IL NE LE FAIT PAS... HOP, VIRÉ
T'ES UNE DRÔLE DE FILLE...
QUAND MÊME... CH'EST DÉGUEULÂCHE
T'ES UNE PETITE NATURE, TU NE SAIS PAS CE QUI EST BON
ON DEVRAIT OBLIGER LES HOMMES À NOUS FAIRE ÇA!
POURQUOI SERAIT-ON LÉSÉES DANS NOTRE PLAISIR SEXUEL CINQ JOURS PAR MOIS !?...
BEN... C'EST LA NATURE

39

43

SURPOPULATION
SOLUTION RADICALE!

MAMAN, LE PLUS BEAU MÉTIER DU MONDE

REISER

45

À TRAVAIL ÉGAL, SALAIRE ÉGAL...

48

CLARA

50

52

53

54

55

56

PHILOSOPHIE PETITE SEMAINE

AUCUNE DIGNITÉ

65

VENTRE CHAUD

AOÛT MOIS DU SEXE

68

69

70

72

DES ABRICOTS À 12 FRANCS!
12
ELLE A BON DOS LA SÉCHERESSE!
AH LA SÉCHERESSE... LA SÉCHERESSE...
12
... ÇA VOUS DONNE DES ENVIES D'UNE BONNE CHATTE BIEN JUTEUSE...
QU'EST-CE QU'ILS ONT, EN CE MOMENT ?...

LES SEINS AU BEURRE NOIR

78

81

VIPÈRE À CORNES, HIBOU À *CUL*

84

TRAVERSER UNE GRANDE VILLE SEULE LA NUIT...

UNE FILLE SEULE LA NUIT, A RÉELLEMENT L'IMPRESSION D'ÊTRE UN PETIT LAPIN DANS LA FORÊT.

ON EMBARQUE AU POSTE UN VENDEUR DE JOURNAUX DANS LA RUE

VOUS GÊNEZ LE PASSAGE

UNE PUTE PARCE QU'ELLE RACOLE DES HOMMES SUR LA VOIE PUBLIQUE

ET ALORS? JE RENDS SERVICE?

▶

PINCÉ!

94

95

97

UNE CHÈVRE VIOLÉE PAR TROIS VOYOUS

99

100

103

104

105

MALAISE
CHEZ LES PHARMACIENS

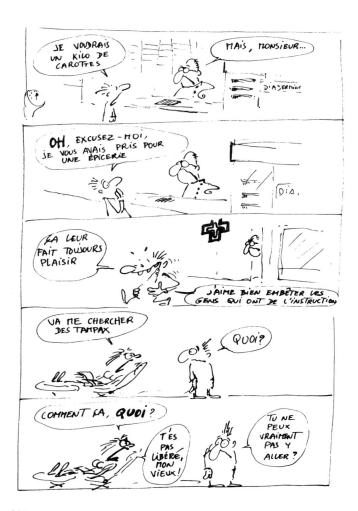

107

MLF PALESTINE VAINCRA

MUSULMANS, MÉFIEZ-VOUS!
LE JOUR OÙ VOS FEMMES
SE RÉVOLTERONT...

GARE À VOS COUILLES!

LA COMMUNION ÉTHYLIQUE
À BAS LES COMMUNIONS !

114

117

LA CASQUETTE À JULES

REISER

PLUS JOLI QUE LES CARTONS

123

HARENGS MIGNONS

LE COIN DES VOLEURS

127

PORNO POSTAL

▶

131

132

133

PROXÉNÈTE FLEURI

136

137

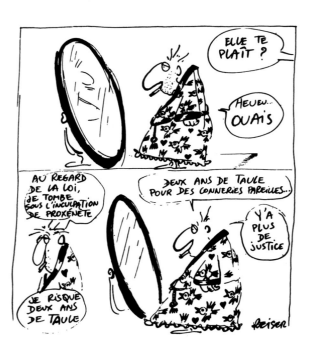

LA TORTURE, C'EST PAS SI SIMPLE...

UNE IDÉE DE MENU
LA DINDE
FARCIE
AU
CON

REISER

ALERTE!

LES VIDE ORDURES TRANSMETTENT DES GERMES INFECTIEUX...

LES PAROIS SONT TAPISSÉES DE STAPHYLOCOQUES

LES ENFANTS DES ETAGES INFÉRIEURS SONT PLUS SOUVENT CONTAMINÉS QUE LES AUTRES

CE QU'ON NE DIT PAS !

C'EST QUE DES MÈRES INDIGNES Y FONT CUIRE DES RAGOUT POUR LEURS GOSSES

143

STEAK GIFLE

PHILOSOPHIE À LA PETITE SEMAINE

COUPS DE PIEDS
DANS LE VENTRE

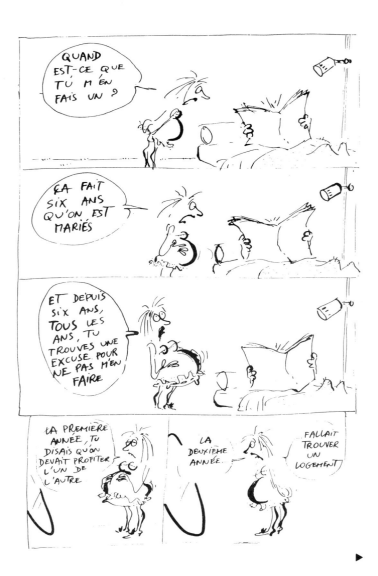

149

150

152

FÊTE DES MÈRES : SAOÛLEZ-VOUS !

REISER

DUR, L'ŒUF DUR...

156

157

UNE MÈRE INDIGNE
DÉCOUPE SON ENFANTE EN RONDELLES

AVEC LE COUTEAU ELECTRIQUE...

QUE JE LUI AVAIS OFFERT POUR LA FÊTE DES MÈRES

ELECTION DE MISS BOURREAU D'ENFANT

REISER

159

SCHRLÛP SCHRLÛP

UNE CARAPACE COMME CELLE DES HUÎTRES PAR EXEMPLE!
QUOI?
IMAGINONS UN INSTANT QUE L'ON TROUVE UN ŒUF DANS UNE COQUILLE SEMBLABLE...
NON!
AVEC UNE PINCE À SUCRE, ON LE FERAIT CUIRE DIRECTEMENT SUR LE GAZ, ÉCONOMIE DE VAISSELLE!
NON
SCHLUUUT
BIOLOGIQUEMENT, ON DEVRAIT BIEN Y ARRIVER UN JOUR!..
NON!

165

L'INQUIÉTUDE DES DINDES GRANDIT

NOËL :

PENSEZ AUX BÊTES ABANDONNÉES

S.P.A

REISER

LA PETITE CHATTE DES PAUVRES

168

169

171

LES FRANÇAIS NE SONT GUÈRES ENTHOUSIASMÉS
PAR LES LÉGUMES SECS

ÇA FAIT
GROSSIR...

ÇA FAIT
PÉTER...

ENCORE
HEUREUX
QUAND ON
PEUT PÉTER...

NOËL !

RELÂCHEZ
VOS MŒURS

REISER

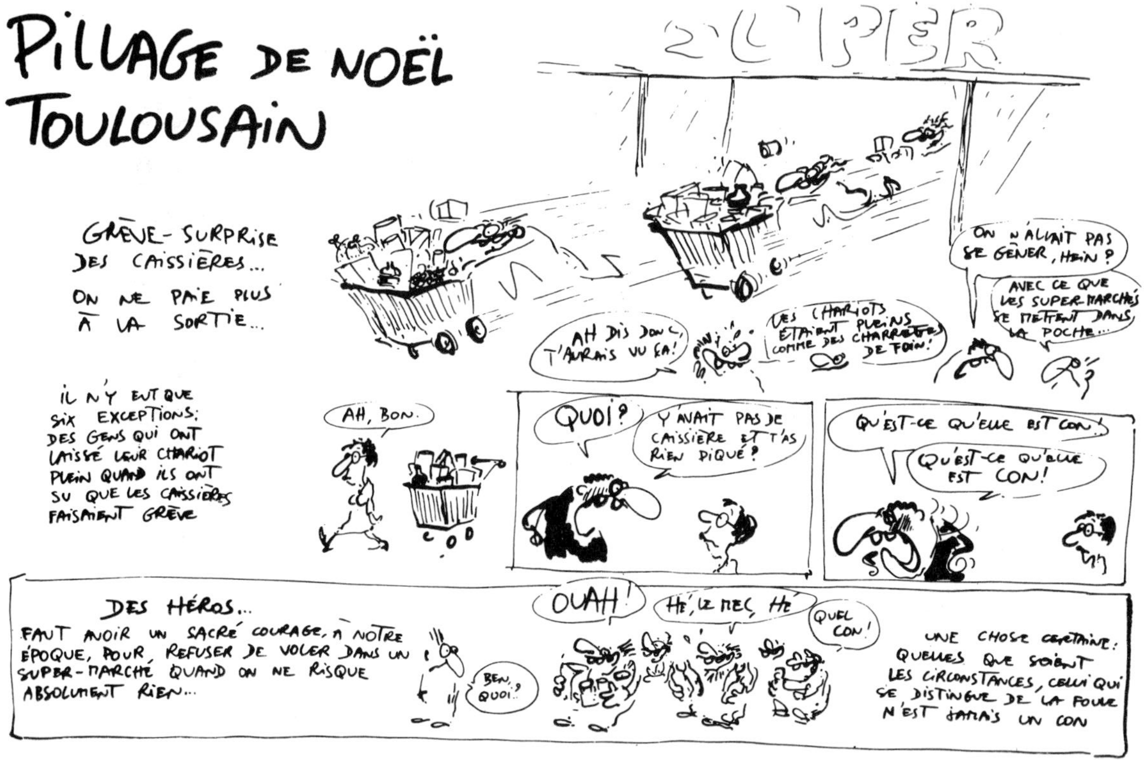
PILLAGE DE NOËL TOULOUSAIN
SUPER
GRÈVE-SURPRISE DES CAISSIÈRES...
ON NE PAIE PLUS À LA SORTIE...
AH DIS DONC, T'AURAIS VU ÇA!
LES CHARIOTS ÉTAIENT PLEINS COMME DES CHARRETTES DE FOIN!
ON N'AVAIT PAS SE GÊNER, HEIN?
AVEC CE QUE LES SUPER-MARCHÉS SE METTENT DANS LA POCHE...
IL N'Y EUT QUE SIX EXCEPTIONS: DES GENS QUI ONT LAISSÉ LEUR CHARIOT PLEIN QUAND ILS ONT SU QUE LES CAISSIÈRES FAISAIENT GRÈVE
AH, BON.
QUOI?
Y AVAIT PAS DE CAISSIÈRE ET T'AS RIEN PIQUÉ?
QU'EST-CE QU'ELLE EST CON!
QU'EST-CE QU'ELLE EST CON!
DES HÉROS...
FAUT AVOIR UN SACRÉ COURAGE, À NOTRE ÉPOQUE, POUR REFUSER DE VOLER DANS UN SUPER-MARCHÉ QUAND ON NE RISQUE ABSOLUMENT RIEN...
BEN, QUOI?
OUAH!
HÉ, LE MEC, HÉ
QUEL CON!
UNE CHOSE CERTAINE: QUELLES QUE SOIENT LES CIRCONSTANCES, CELUI QUI SE DISTINGUE DE LA FOULE N'EST JAMAIS UN CON

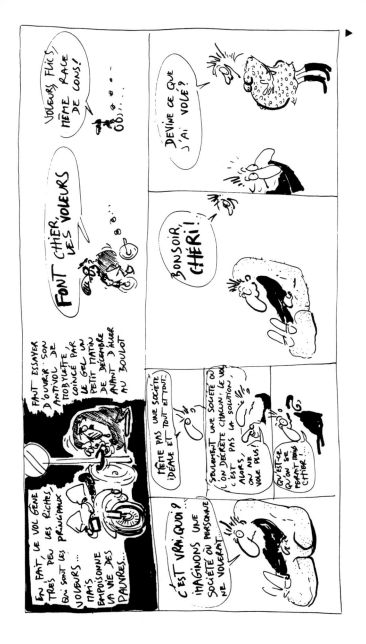

ANNÉE DE LA FEMME:
LES HOMMES DEVRONT RÉPONDRE
À TOUTES LEURS QUESTIONS.

183

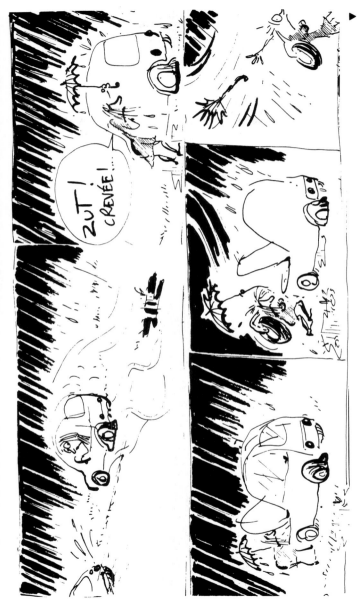

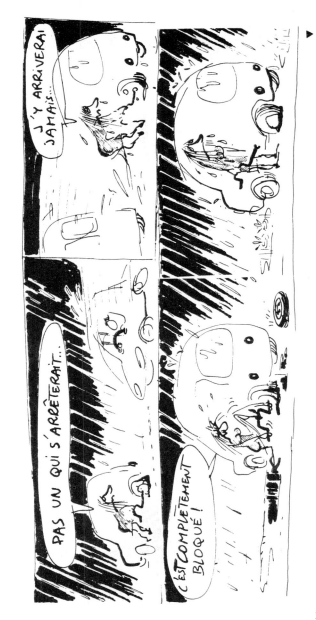

187

189

191

194

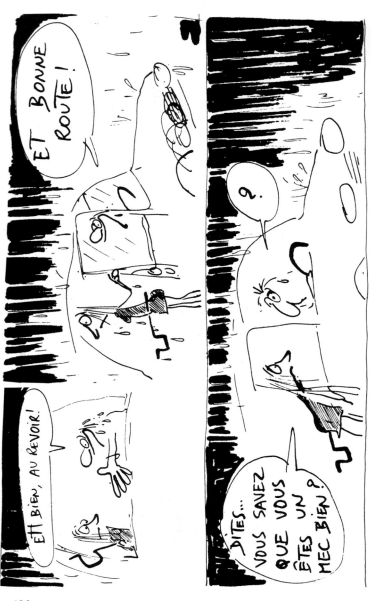

197

198

DU MÊME AUTEUR

*Cet ouvrage a été reproduit
et achevé d'imprimer par l'Imprimerie Pollina
à Luçon, le 12 octobre 1993.
Dépôt légal : octobre 1993.
1ᵉʳ depôt légal dans la collection : novembre 1988.
Numéro d'imprimeur : 63932.*

ISBN 2-07-038089-0 / Imprimé en France.
Précédemment publié par les éditions Albin Michel.
ISBN 2-226-01372-5.

BRITISH STUFF

BRITISH STUFF

First published in 2013
This revised edition copyright © Geoff Hall and Kamila Kasperowicz, 2016

Summersdale Publishers Ltd
46 West Street
Chichester
West Sussex
PO19 1RP
UK

www.summersdale.com

Printed and bound in China

ISBN: 978-1-84953-849-7

Substantial discounts on bulk quantities of Summersdale books are available to corporations, professional associations and other organisations. For details contact Nicky Douglas by telephone: +44 (0) 1243 756902, fax: +44 (0) 1243 786300 or email: nicky@summersdale.com.

BRITISH
STUFF

101 OBJECTS THAT MAKE BRITAIN GREAT

GEOFF HALL & KAMILA KASPEROWICZ

summersdale

INTRODUCTION

This book was inspired by a love of physical objects: things that you can see, touch, smell and in some cases taste. Not old objects, but the ones with which we are most familiar. Objects appeal to our senses, but they often have stories to tell as well: stories about how they came into being, about why they have survived and how their significance has changed over time.

In a globalised world where new ideas are communicated instantly, more and more of the objects we use are international in nature. It is often difficult to attribute an individual object to any one nation.

The iPhone, for example, was designed by a British designer, Jonathan Ive, but it is mostly assembled in China and marketed by an American company, Apple. Not just that, but you are as likely to find it in the hands of an office worker in Shanghai or an IT professional in Mumbai as in those of a lawyer in New York or a banker in London.

For over 400 years, Britain has been an international power and many of the ideas and products which originated here, especially sports like cricket and tennis, have been exported around the world. Britain has in turn imported many things from other countries – from tea to wallpaper – and adapted them to meet its own needs.

All this may lead us to conclude that there could not possibly be very much left that is distinctively British. And yet, when visitors come to Britain and Britons visit other countries, they immediately recognise differences. It is not just about the buildings or the language. It is about the clothes, hats and shoes that people wear, the food they eat, the transport they use and the objects they employ in their daily lives.

Alongside this there is a growing interest in what has come to be known as 'material culture', an awareness that this 'stuff' should not simply be dismissed as mere examples of a shallow 'materialist' world, but recognised as objects that tell valuable and interesting stories about twenty-first-century people and their lives.

The objects that have been included in this book have been chosen using four main criteria:

Firstly, the objects selected all have some distinctively British flavour or characteristic. They are things that would strike a visitor to Britain as unusual or different from what they would find at home.

Secondly, we have included only objects that have some element of man-made design, so you will not find primroses or oak trees here, even though some might consider them quintessentially British.

Thirdly, the objects are all in current use, not objects from a museum. It is true that some may only be used by a minority, often older people, or be more heavily used in one part of the country than another, but they will still be in regular use and recognised as such. Some may be luxury products, like the Rolls-Royce Phantom, available only to a privileged few, but most will not.

Finally, the objects help build a broader picture of life in Britain today. Not a complete one of course, because Britain is one of the most multicultural countries in the world and many first- and second-generation immigrants who are now British citizens will have their own sets of distinctive 'stuff'.

We have excluded buildings and landmarks, so no Buckingham Palace or Anne Hathaway's cottage, no Paddington Station or Houses of Parliament. What we wanted to capture are the things that people can see anywhere in Britain, that British people use every day, and that above all contribute in some way to their own sense of identity.

MINI

The Mini is one of those rare products that has evolved over time from functional workhorse to fashion icon. It was designed in the late 1950s by the British Motor Corporation as a practical, fuel-efficient family car. At that time, three-wheel bubble cars were the only choice for motorists who needed a small, economical car. The Mini was revolutionary because its transverse engine, front-wheel-drive layout left plenty of space for four passengers, with luggage, in a car just 3 metres long.

To begin with sales were slow, as the Mini gained a reputation for being unreliable and complicated to fix. But then, in the early 1960s, two things happened. First the Mini Cooper proved to be a great (and unexpected) success in rallying. Then a number of celebrities, including the actor Peter Sellers and the Beatles, were seen in Minis. It soon became associated with the swinging London fashion and music scene of the 1960s, and its starring role in the hit film *The Italian Job* in 1969 cemented its success.

The Mini had established itself as a style icon, and many of its distinctive design features have been carried on in the newer MINI – now owned by the German company BMW, but still partly built in Britain – which was launched in 2001 and is now exported all over the world.

Owners of the newer MINI seem to form the same kind of bond with their cars that drivers of the old one did. Every year owners of both older and newer Minis are invited to take part in 'The Italian Job, a driving adventure' from Italy to the UK, which harks back to the 1969 film, and whose proceeds are donated to children's charities.

"

Its starring role in the hit film The Italian Job *in 1969 cemented its success*

621 AOK

LEA & PERRINS WORCESTERSHIRE SAUCE

Whilst many companies sell a product under the title of Worcestershire (pronounced *woos-tah-shir*) sauce, the original – The Original & Genuine Lea & Perrins Worcestershire Sauce, to give it its full name – is the one illustrated here. Still made in Worcester at the Midland Road factory set up to produce it in 1897, Lea & Perrins is often added to savoury dishes like casseroles, chilli con carne and Welsh rarebit, but is probably best known for its starring role alongside vodka and tomato juice in the Bloody Mary cocktail.

Messrs Lea and Perrins were pharmacists who owned a shop in Worcester. The story goes that in 1835 a local nobleman returning from Bengal gave them a recipe that he had brought back from there. The two chemists followed the recipe, but agreed that the sauce tasted terrible. Instead of pouring it away, though, they bottled it and left it in their cellars. When they rediscovered the jars some time later they tasted it once again and discovered that it had fermented into a delicious savoury sauce.

In 1837, they started to sell the product under the now familiar Lea & Perrins name. Within six years their energetic marketing campaigns had increased sales dramatically to some 14,500 bottles a year – a significant amount for a product which is used only sparingly.

Lea & Perrins were keen to protect their secret recipe and in 1906 took one rival to court, claiming that they had the exclusive right to make Worcestershire sauce. The court found against Lea & Perrins, but did permit them the exclusive right to call theirs 'original and genuine', a phrase which still appears prominently on the label today.

> **"**
> *In 1835 a local nobleman returning from Bengal gave them a recipe*
> **"**

POSTAGE STAMP

Until the early nineteenth century, there was no simple way to send a letter in Britain, or anywhere else for that matter. Postage was not paid by the sender but by the recipient of the letter, which meant that if the recipient refused to pay then there was no way to recover the cost and, furthermore, if the sender did not have to pay, he or she had no incentive to minimise the size and weight of the letter.

In 1837, Victoria became Queen of England, and at around the same time an Englishman, Sir Rowland Hill, produced a document entitled 'Post Office Reform: Its Importance and Practicability', paving the way for the postal system which now operates in most countries around the world.

Rowland Hill's idea was to charge the same fee regardless of distance travelled, with postage paid by the sender. At the same time he introduced the idea of a postage stamp: a pre-gummed piece of black paper showing the agreed standard charge for all letters, one penny.

Every British stamp since the first 'Penny Black' in May 1840 has borne the head of the reigning monarch, always in profile. As these were the very first stamps anywhere, no one thought to put the name of the country on British stamps. So, even though postage stamps are not a uniquely British phenomenon, to this day Britain remains the only country in the world not to carry the name of the country on its stamps.

BLACKPOOL ROCK

Blackpool rock: a rod of hard, boiled sugar about 30 cm long and 2–3 cm in diameter, pink on the outside, white on the inside, with lettering running through its centre, flavoured with peppermint or spearmint.

It is one of those rare objects that makes you ask: how do they make that? How do they get the lettering to run all the way down a stick of rock? Although some parts of the rock-making process can be handled by machine, much of it is still done by hand, especially the forming of the individual letters which are carefully rolled, stretched and twisted, one letter at a time, and then combined to form the finished word while the mixture is still warm.

In the north of England it was Blackpool that became the supreme seaside resort. Over the course of the nineteenth century it grew from a small village into the prime holiday destination for the industrial working classes of Lancashire and Yorkshire. In 1801, the town had a population of 473; a century later it had grown a hundredfold – to over 47,000. What changed its fortunes was the arrival of the railway, which allowed industrial workers from Manchester and Leeds to reach it easily. Blackpool responded by creating cheap accommodation, entertainment and food. When the famous Blackpool Tower was built in 1894 it was the tallest building in the country. And, of course, they made rock. Blackpool rock, still made there to this day.

HILLE SERIES E CHAIR

If you visit any school assembly hall, company restaurant or village hall in Britain you will likely encounter one of the many versions of the Hille stackable polypropylene chair. Designed by Robin Day in 1963, it is thought that up to 20 million have been produced since then. Cheap to produce, strong, lightweight, hard-wearing and easy to stack, the Hille chair is a rare example of a design icon so effective and ubiquitous that it has become almost invisible. Day's designs reflect the time in which he was working. Instead of the heavy and often cumbersome furniture designs which went before, Day's chairs were more delicate, with thinner legs, and they used the minimum of materials (an important factor in the lingering austerity of post-war Britain).

Although the polypropylene chair now looks commonplace, it was radical for its time. The brief from Hille called for a low-cost stacking chair, which could be mass-produced and used in a wide range of situations. Polypropylene itself had only been invented (by an Italian, Giulio Natta) nine years earlier and few companies had the expertise to injection-mould it. The chair's folded edges not only gave it extra strength but also made it easier to pick up and slot into place when stacking. The lip on the sides allowed each chair to sit directly on top of the one below, stopping the stack from leaning over as it got higher.

The original design, known as the Polyside chair, was replaced by the Series E in 1972. It is true that although the chair is recognised as a design classic, not all users consider it a success. One online design blogger described it caustically as 'the design equivalent of radioactivity'.

"The design equivalent of radioactivity"

ANGLEPOISE LAMP

The Anglepoise lamp is an iconic design which has found its way around the world, but its origins and design retain uniquely British characteristics. Designed and developed not by a professional designer, but by an engineer, the Anglepoise was not the product of any coherent business-led R&D programme.

In 1932, an automotive engineer, George Carwardine, patented a new type of spring which could retain its position after being stretched or compressed. Carwardine owned a company in the west of England which specialised in vehicle suspension systems, but it seems the research that led to the Anglepoise lamp was largely undertaken by him out of curiosity. Aware of basic engineering principles and also the constant tension principle associated with the human arm, Carwardine spent two years developing what would become the Anglepoise. He originally planned to call it the Equipoise, but was unable to register that name. His plan was that the lamp would be used purely for industrial and assembly work.

In 1934, he licensed the light, but not to a lighting manufacturer. Instead, the company of Herbert Terry & Sons, a manufacturer based at Redditch in Worcestershire which supplied springs, took up its development and marketing. In 1937, the patent was sold to the Norwegian lighting designer Jacob Jacobsen, who went on to create his own variant, the Luxor L-1, which achieved success in its own right.

Not only does the lamp work exceptionally well, providing well-directed light, a big part of its appeal must also lie in its resemblance to a human companion; the Anglepoise has a strangely benign appearance, like a hooded monk peeking encouragingly over your shoulder while you work.

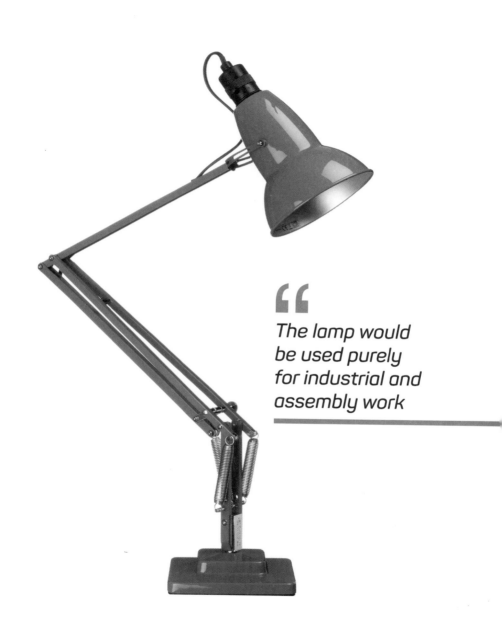

> **"**
> *The lamp would
> be used purely
> for industrial and
> assembly work*

CRUMPET

A crumpet is a circular-shaped bread-like unsweetened cake made from flour and yeast. It usually has holes in the top, which result from adding baking powder. Although it is easy to find recipes to make your own crumpets, often people buy part-cooked crumpets at the supermarket and then toast them or heat them under a grill at home.

Many people would consider a crumpet an ideal snack with their afternoon tea, but what they choose to eat on their toasted crumpet is much more varied. Sweet toppings might include honey, golden syrup or jam, whilst savoury accompaniments such as cheese, Marmite or a poached egg will be favoured by others.

There is also a regional variant of the crumpet called the pikelet. It is usually made from the same kind of batter as a crumpet, and in some parts of England, for example in the Birmingham area, a pikelet is simply a crumpet without holes. In other parts, such as around Manchester, a pikelet has holes, but is wider and thinner than a crumpet. In Wales a pikelet is very different from a crumpet and resembles what in Scotland is called a pancake and in most parts of England is called a Scotch pancake. We hope this is all perfectly clear.

Before the rise of feminism – say, before the 1970s – it was not uncommon for men to refer to an attractive woman as 'crumpet' and for a woman who was both attractive and intelligent to be referred to as 'thinking man's crumpet', but if you use the word crumpet now to refer to a woman you will seem very out of date and rather sexist.

> **"** *In the Birmingham area,*
> *a pikelet is simply a*
> *crumpet without holes*

K6 TELEPHONE KIOSK

In 1924, the Post Office launched a competition to produce a new telephone kiosk. The winning design – called the K2 (Kiosk No. 2) – was created by Sir Giles Gilbert Scott, the architect who also designed the Anglican Cathedral in Liverpool and London's Battersea Power Station.

Scott originally intended his kiosk to be painted silver, with a blue-green interior. However, the Post Office decided to paint them red, so that they would be easier to see in an emergency. The colour, however, was not their biggest problem. The K2 was big and expensive to make, so in 1935 Scott came up with a revised version of the K2, which was smaller, lighter and cheaper to build – designated the K6.

The K6 kiosk appeared in 1936, followed by a more vandal-proof version in 1939. In the 1980s the Post Office was privatised and the new company, British Telecom, tried to introduce alternative modernist designs in glass and steel featuring its new pale grey logo, but a public outcry meant that numbers of the red kiosks were preserved.

Today, over 90 per cent of adults in the United Kingdom now have a mobile phone, so, as much as people love the iconic red kiosks, few actually use them for telephony. However, the K6 still has its uses: in Kingston upon Thames, artist David Mach toppled 12 kiosks against one another to create an artwork titled 'Out of Order', and graffiti artist Banksy had fun with another, cutting and rewelding it to form the impression that it had been killed by the axe that protruded from it. You can see it in his film *Exit through the Giftshop*.

Scott originally intended his kiosk to be painted silver

BARBOUR JACKET

The Barbour jacket is a Range Rover without the wheels... or an engine: it speaks of a rugged, outdoor life in the country even when it is cruising round the streets of Kensington or Chelsea. It may never get anywhere close to a fishing stream or a grouse moor in Scotland, but it makes you believe that it (and its wearer) could survive there just as easily if it had to. Wear it in Knightsbridge in the week; take it to the country at the weekend.

However, the company in fact started out in the north-east of England, in South Shields in 1894, catering to the sailors and dockyard workers of Tyneside, who bought Barbour's waterproof oilskin jackets for strictly practical reasons – because they kept them warm and dry, and because they were durable. Over time it was natural for Barbour's market to extend to other activities that required people to be outdoors in

all weathers: motorcyclists, horse riders, leisure fishermen and other country sports enthusiasts.

Barbour – which remains family-owned – has made moves to shake off its traditional image and widen its appeal to a new, younger clientele, engaging in collaborations with designers like Alice Temperley and with fashion companies like Paul Smith's R. Newbold brand to create a cooler urban streetwear collection.

Fashion may be the future for Barbour, but the joy of it is that it works. Function precedes fashion. Its shooting jacket features high pockets for easy access to shotgun cartridges; its motorcycle jacket will withstand wind-buffeting. Just as the Range Rover boasts the highest level of off-road capability (even if never required by most of its customers), so the Barbour is designed to see off the worst the British climate can throw at it.

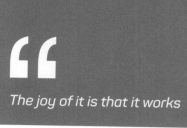

"

The joy of it is that it works

HOT-WATER BOTTLE

'Continental people have sex lives; the English have hot-water bottles.' That was the view of the humorist George Mikes, who came to live in London from his native country, Hungary, in the 1930s.

A hot-water bottle is a container filled with hot water and sealed with a screw-in stopper, used to provide warmth, usually in bed. In the event of injury it can also be held against a sore part of the body for pain relief.

People used containers for warmth in bed in Britain as early as the sixteenth century. The earliest versions were metal and a maid or servant would fill the pan with hot charcoal from the embers of a log fire and place it in the bedclothes some time before their master or mistress was planning to retire to bed.

In the 1960s, my father had a heavy pottery bottle, which he filled with hot water every night in winter. It worked fine back then, as his bed had sheets and blankets tucked in under the mattress, which held the bottle in place. He has moved on, like most British people, to using a loose duvet on his bed, so no longer uses the old bottle.

George Mikes made his original joke about the British attitude to sex and hot-water bottles in 1946 and, when asked about it in the 1970s, he agreed that things had moved on. But only because the English had discovered electric blankets in the meantime.

KENDAL MINT CAKE

According to popular legend, the recipe for Kendal mint cake was originally discovered by accident.

A confectioner called Joseph Wiper who lived in Kendal, in Cumbria, was intending to make clear ('glacier') mints but took his eye off the cooking pan for a few minutes. When he looked back he noticed that the mixture had become cloudy. He poured it out into a tray and the result was mint cake. Wiper (who later emigrated to Canada) started making the mint cake at his small factory at Ferney Green in Kendal in 1869. Initially, the product was only sold to locals but soon the railway encouraged sales further afield.

There was a second big break a few decades later, in the early twentieth century, when Kendal mint cake came to be prized as a concentrated source of energy much valued by explorers and mountaineers. The polar explorer Ernest Shackleton took it with him on his 1914–17 Trans-Antarctic Expedition and later Edmund Hillary included it in the high-altitude packs used on his 1953 ascent of Everest. This latter fact is still commemorated today on the back of packs of Romney's Kendal mint cake, where a member of the successful 1953 expedition is quoted as saying: 'It was easily the most popular item on our high-altitude ration – our only criticism was that we did not have enough of it.'

Today, Kendal mint cake remains a popular energy source for walkers and climbers and is sold all over the country and abroad.

STINKING BISHOP CHEESE

There are over 700 different cheeses in Britain, so trying to select just one to represent them all is hard. The obvious choice might have been Cheddar, since it accounts for half of all the cheese consumed in the country, and its origins are undoubtedly British, emanating as it does from the village of Cheddar in Somerset. Instead, though, we chose the wonderfully named Stinking Bishop, which is only made by one small dairy in Gloucestershire.

Voted Britain's smelliest cheese in 2009, the Press Association reported that 'the Stinking Bishop made by Charles Martell of Martell and Son in Gloucestershire blew the judges away and was described as smelling like a rugby club changing room'.

In spite of its name, Stinking Bishop does not actually taste anything like as pungent as it smells. Nor is it called Stinking Bishop because of its smell. It is a soft cheese whose rind is soaked every four weeks during the maturing process in a pear cider (perry) made from the local Stinking Bishop pear. The pear is properly named Moorcroft (after the farm it originated on), but was given the additional name after a man who bred it, a Mr Bishop, who was either reputed to have an ugly temper or to have a relaxed attitude to hygiene, depending on which source you believe. Its flavour has been variously described as sweetish, fruity and buttery.

In 2005, Stinking Bishop gained additional fame when it played a starring role in the Wallace & Gromit film, *The Curse of the Were-Rabbit*, in which it was used to revive Wallace, bringing him back from the dead.

Sales of Stinking Bishop rose fivefold after the film came out, no doubt due to its miraculous life-giving properties.

> **"**
> *Described as smelling like a rugby club changing room*
> **"**

Stinking
Bishop

Rind Washed in Perry
Full Fat semi-soft cheese
Vegetarian rennet
Charles Martell & Son Ltd
HUNTS COURT FARM
DYMOCK
GLOUCESTERSHIRE
ENGLAND

MARMITE

Marmite is a thick, dark brown paste, with a strong, savoury flavour, usually eaten on toast or crumpets. The name comes from the French word *marmite*, meaning a large cooking pot, a picture of which appears on the label. The jar itself is something of a design classic – distinctively shaped to resemble a casserole.

Made from yeast extract, Marmite is a by-product of beer brewing and so the first plant was sited alongside the Bass Brewery in Burton-on-Trent. Introduced in 1902, it was so popular that, just five years later, the then family-owned company opened a further plant in London.

Constantly innovative, the manufacturers of Marmite leave no stone unturned in coming up with new Marmite-related ideas. In celebration of the Queen's Diamond Jubilee in 2012, the company renamed its product 'Ma'amite' for a limited period. It has also introduced a specially shaped knife (yes, called a Marmife) designed to help you get the very last bit of Marmite out of the jar.

Because of its distinctive, strong flavour, people tend to either love or hate Marmite and the manufacturers have exploited its ability to polarise opinion by running marketing campaigns that play on the 'love it or hate it' theme. Marmite is now so entrenched in British life that the word Marmite is used generally to describe anything which people either love or hate.

"The jar itself is something of a design classic"

POLICEMAN'S HELMET

The British police service dates back to 1829 when it was formed in London by Sir Robert Peel, and the early policemen came to be known as 'bobbies' or 'peelers'.

From the start they were armed only with a wooden truncheon, together with a rattle (and later a whistle) in order to attract attention. The colour of their uniform – dark blue – was also selected to distinguish the police from the military, who typically wore red at the time. Modern British police only carry guns in extreme circumstances or at sensitive locations such as airports and embassies.

The design of the police helmet followed the form of the German *Pickelhaube*, the spiked helmet worn by German officers up to the time of World War One. Surprisingly, it has survived numerous moves to modernise the police uniform.

Today the traditional headgear of the policeman is reserved for officers patrolling the street (the 'bobbies on the beat') and for obvious practical reasons it is replaced by a peaked cap for officers on mobile patrol in a car. Policemen charged with dealing with crowds and riots are now also better equipped, with purpose-made riot helmets and visors.

In the days when men and women almost always wore hats outside of the home, Britain was a centre of hat-making, but today that industry has declined sharply.

> The design of the police helmet follows the form of the German Pickelhaube

COMIC SEASIDE POSTCARD

Until the 1960s, very few British people went abroad for their holidays. Instead, most would head for the coast to one of the many seaside towns like Blackpool, Brighton or Skegness. By modern standards these were unsophisticated places, but there was still fun to be had during a break from repetitive factory life, which was the lot of most workers at the time. The seaside postcard was part of that fun; the message you sent home to friends to assure them that you were having a great time, often in spite of the wet English climate.

The heyday of the English seaside postcard coincided with the peak in popularity of seaside resorts in the first half of the twentieth century, so it went into decline in the 1960s and 1970s, when British holidaymakers started heading for the more reliable climate of Spain or went in search of the gastronomic treats offered by France.

The survival of the comic postcard into the twenty-first century is almost entirely due to one company, Bamforth of Yorkshire, the same firm that initiated comic postcards in the early twentieth century.

The comic seaside postcard may now look quaint, as it harks back to an age when sex was considered a bit naughty, and certainly not to be talked about in polite company. But as sexual attitudes have become more liberal, the frisson of childish naughtiness that is inseparable from these comic cards has largely been removed, but you will still find them bringing a smile on the seafronts of English seaside towns.

DECKCHAIR

The deckchair is a masterpiece of elegant design, simple in concept, cheap to make, easy to store and comfortable to sit in. Constructed from as few as 11 pieces of wood, a straight length of fabric and a handful of fastenings, the deckchair provides a comfortable and relaxing way to enjoy the sunshine on a warm summer's afternoon, especially on a beach by the sea.

Folding chairs were recorded in Egyptian times, but it was in the late nineteenth century that the modern deckchair became popular. John Thomas Moore patented his design for a folding chair in 1886. As the name 'deckchair' suggests, it was popular for sitting out on the deck of an ocean liner as it transported its passengers to various parts of the then flourishing British Empire. It also became associated with the healthy sea air enjoyed on deck, and its light weight and compact dimensions when folded made it ideal for storage on a ship.

The deckchair was soon adopted on beaches and piers around Britain's coastline. Once again it scored because it was comfortable and easy to fold away for storage at the end of the day or over the winter.

It has also found its way into a common phrase. If someone tells you a proposed activity is like 'rearranging the deckchairs on the Titanic', you will know that they mean it to be too trivial to help deal with the real issue at hand.

TWENTY-POUND NOTE

The first notes in pounds sterling were issued in 1696, making sterling the world's oldest currency still in use. Until 1971, the pound was divided into 20 shillings, each shilling equalling 12 old pence, but in 1971 the current decimal system was introduced, greatly simplifying things. So one pound now is made up of 100 new pence. The pound – along with the US Dollar, the Euro and the Japanese Yen – is one of the four most commonly traded currencies, and it is the third most commonly held currency in global reserves.

The twenty-pound note was introduced in 1745, but was discontinued during World War Two due to fears of a German attempt to issue fake currency, and it was only reintroduced 30 years later, in 1970.

All sterling notes show the picture of the reigning monarch on one side and a historical figure on the back. As Queen Elizabeth II has been on the British throne since 1952, all current banknotes show her head on the front.

The custom of depicting historical figures on the reverse of banknotes began with the image of William Shakespeare being used on the twenty-pound note in 1970. Many other famous Britons have featured on successive issues, including Michael Faraday (the English chemist and physicist best known for his experiments on electromagnetism), Edward Elgar (the composer best known for his *Enigma Variations* and *Pomp and Circumstance Marches*) and Adam Smith (the father of modern economics).

ROYAL ASCOT LADIES' DAY HAT

There has been horse racing at Ascot for over 300 years. The race course was established by Queen Anne in 1711 and the Gold Cup, a race for horses aged four years or more, celebrated its 200th anniversary in 2007. That race is the main event of Ladies' Day, and Ladies' Day is itself the racing and social highlight of the Royal Ascot racing meet (an event that is spread over five days in June), when fashion and Ascot hats in particular come out in force.

Royal Ascot is the top social event of the British racing and royal calendars. The crowds turn out, not just to watch the horse racing, but to see the Queen and other members of the Royal Family at leisure, engaged in an activity that they enjoy. For visitors expecting to gain entry into the Royal Enclosure there is a very strict dress code. For ladies this specifies that: 'Dresses and skirts should be of modest length defined as falling just above the knee or longer... Hats should be worn; a headpiece which has a base of 4 in. (10 cm) or more in diameter is acceptable as an alternative to a hat.'

The hats that ladies wear range from the elegant to the bizarre and flamboyant, usually the more outrageous the better if the intention is to get noticed. Ladies' Day at Royal Ascot is an opportunity for women of all means to preen, be seen and if possible be photographed. Hat designer Ilda Di Vico, pictured here, wore one of her own elaborate creations, a series of red and black hoops, with small ladybirds, worn stylishly down over the right eye.

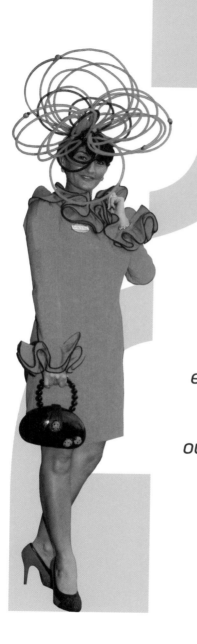

The hats ladies wear range from the elegant to the bizarre and flamboyant, usually the more outrageous the better

MORGAN THREE WHEELER

Morgan is a small, family-owned British manufacturer of very eccentric sports cars, most of which look as though they date back to the 1930s. At a time – over the last 20 years – when UK manufacturing in general has declined sharply, Morgan has gone from strength to strength. In 1990 it made just 400 cars, but by 2011 this had grown to 1,000 and its order book is still full.

The first Morgan was produced in 1910 and only went into production because of favourable response to its design. That first car was also a three-wheeler, inspired as much by bicycle design as by cars. What made the Morgan Three Wheeler exceptional was its lightness, which made it unusually quick, rivalling many much more powerful cars.

Whilst the new Morgan Three Wheeler is, in many ways, a reinvention of the original, it also has some neatly quirky postmodern touches; for example, the starter button replicates the bomb-release button from a Eurofighter jet. Buyers can choose paintwork in the style of a World War Two Spitfire, or of a hot rod, or they can opt to add decals of retro pin-ups in the style of a B-52 bomber. And it is also very quick, going from 0–60 in 4.5 seconds and having a top speed of more than 120 mph.

Like other design classics you do not buy a Morgan for its outright performance or for its practical value. You buy it because of the way it makes you feel.

"" Inspired as much by bicycle design as by cars

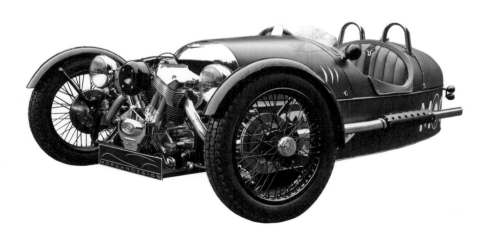

THE BRITISH ISLES SEA AREAS MAP

The shipping forecast is an integral and reassuring part of life for many of the ten million listeners to BBC Radio 4; so important, in fact, that it was included in the Opening Ceremony for the 2012 Olympic Games in London.

Broadcast four times a day, the shipping forecast is issued by the UK Meteorological (or Met) Office to provide vital weather information to shipping around the coastlines of the British Isles. Sailors and fishermen depend on this forecast, and access to it on long-wave radio ensures that they can remain informed even if more modern systems such as radar, GPS and their own ship-to-shore radio should fail.

Key to its understanding is the Sea Areas map which shows the location of the individual zones around Britain, and an understanding of where they are adds to the strange pleasure that many derive from the shipping forecast itself. Of course, neither you nor most of the other listeners need to know what the weather conditions are like in the North Sea west of Norway (that would be in sea areas North Utsire or South Utsire), but that is not the point. As you snuggle under your bedclothes to stay warm in the early hours it will greatly add to your pleasure to know that it is blowing a Force 9 gale in south-east Iceland.

The interest that many British people have in the shipping forecast reflects the nation's fascination with its ever-changing weather. Any overseas visitor to Britain can be assured that the weather is a perfect subject with which to initiate casual conversation.

> *It will greatly add to your pleasure to know that it is blowing a Force 9 gale in south-east Iceland*

'FOLK THE BANKS' T-SHIRT

In 2008, the British banking system, like many others around the world, came close to collapse, almost destroyed by the over-availability of credit and the recklessness of its bankers. And because London is such a prominent centre of global finance it felt the fallout as intensely as anywhere.

Reprising his role as the graphic art leader of the anti-establishment movement was Jamie Reid, whose cover for a fundraising music album titled 'Folk the Banks' was quickly taken up as a T-shirt design. Reid had been here before, 40 years earlier…

In the mid 1970s, pop music in Britain was largely split between the earnest post-hippy rock groups like Pink Floyd or Led Zeppelin and the glam rock scene of T. Rex and David Bowie. But in 1976 a new musical force punched its way into the headlines: punk. Led by the Sex Pistols, punk was the complete opposite of mainstream music; it was disrespectful, ugly, foul-mouthed, angry, discordant and nihilistic.

At the heart of this anarchistic force was the graphic artist Jamie Reid. He designed the covers for the most famous Pistols records, including their one studio album, *Never Mind the Bollocks*. Reid took establishment images like the Queen's head and defaced them, adding lettering cut from newspapers to create the effect of a ransom note – precisely the aggressive and beyond-the-law values that the Sex Pistols wanted to be known for.

If punk personified Britain in the 1970s, then it is the greed of bankers and the ensuing banking crisis that characterised the first decade of the twenty-first century. True to his principles, Jamie Reid continues to use his unique style of collage to produce art that challenges the establishment.

> *Disrespectful, ugly, foul-mouthed, angry, discordant and nihilistic*

A–Z STREET MAP

The first A–Z street map was created by Phyllis Pearsall in 1935. Legend has it that she was trying to find her way to a party in the London district of Belgravia, armed with the latest map she could find, but, as that map was more than 15 years old, she got lost and never got there.

Spurred by this experience, Phyllis decided to make a completely new map of London. To do this she would get up at 5 a.m. every day, working for up to 18 hours a day, mapping and indexing every one of London's 23,000 streets and walking a total of 3,000 miles.

At the end of this labour, however, she was unable to persuade any of the existing book publishers to take her book on so decided to publish it herself by founding the Geographers' Map Company.

She published *The A–Z Atlas and Guide to London and Suburbs* in 1936 and today almost anyone who lives in London will have a recent copy on their bookshelf or computer.

Her legend has sadly been called into doubt by recent researchers, who point out that the A–Z was not the first documented map of London and that they actually existed as far back as the seventeenth century. They also point out that Phyllis's father had himself previously set up a mapping company, so this was perhaps not quite the pioneering venture it sounds. As for the claims about the distance she walked, they point out that much of the information would have been available at borough town halls. The legend is much more interesting, though, so we'll stick with that, and there is little doubt in any event that her version was more comprehensive and more accurate than anything that had gone before.

She would get up at 5 a.m. every day, working for up to 18 hours a day

UNION JACK CUSHION

The British flag, known as the Union Jack or Union Flag, is one of the most distinctive national flags in the world. The current layout dates back to 1801, to the Union of Great Britain and Ireland.

The design is distinctive because it was created by combining the national flags of Scotland, England and Ireland: the white diagonal cross of Saint Andrew on its blue background for Scotland, the red vertical cross of Saint George for England and the red diagonal cross of Saint Patrick for Ireland. Although Wales is also one of the four nations making up the United Kingdom, it is not represented in the current design of the Union Jack. Meanwhile, some people in Scotland remain keen on pushing for full independence, so the Union Jack could change beyond present recognition in the coming years.

One reason for the enduring iconic status of the Union Jack is its association with youth culture and fashion. At the height of Beatlemania in the early 1960s London's Carnaby Street became a focal point for post-war exuberance. Musicians adopted the Union Jack, notably Pete Townshend, who wore a Union Jack jacket on The Who's first album cover, and later the punks who wore Vivienne Westwood-designed Union Jack T-shirts in the 1970s. Freddie Mercury, Oasis and the Spice Girls have all given further exposure to the design.

Today you can find the Union Jack on all kinds of clothing and home accessories, including bedding, mugs, teapots and cushions. And to add a touch of style to your kitchen attire when demonstrating your cooking skills, why not try a Union Jack apron?

HOT CROSS BUN

A hot cross bun is a sweet spiced bun made with raisins and candied fruits, traditionally only made in the run-up to Easter, but increasingly available at other times of year as well. The cross on the top symbolises the crucifixion of Christ, which is why the hot cross bun was traditionally associated with Good Friday, when the buns would be cut in half and eaten either cold or toasted, usually with butter.

In spite of their strong links to Christianity, some believe that people were making hot cross buns long before the religion came to Britain. They are certainly now a well-established tradition, even featuring in a children's nursery rhyme:

> *Hot cross buns,*
> *Hot cross buns,*
> *One ha' penny,*
> *Two ha' penny,*
> *Hot cross buns.*

There are also superstitions associated with hot cross buns. For example, one of them says that a hot cross bun baked on Good Friday will not go mouldy during the subsequent year.

In London there is a pub called The Widow's Son, where a woman once lived whose son was due home on leave from the Royal Navy. Expecting him home on Good Friday, she was heartbroken when he did not arrive. Living in hope, she would bake a new bun for him every Easter, adding to those she had kept from previous years. When she died these buns were found in a net hanging from a beam in her cottage, and ever since the pub was opened in 1848 the tradition has been maintained by each subsequent landlord, with a sailor from the Royal Navy placing a new bun in the net each year.

*A hot cross bun
baked on Good Friday
will not go mouldy*

ORANGE MARMALADE

It is said that marmalade-making in Britain started in Scotland, though different forms of marmalade had been produced earlier in other countries. It comes from the Portuguese word, *marmelo*, meaning quince, but these earlier marmalades had the consistency of a paste, unlike the chunky texture of modern-day marmalade.

According to legend, a ship carrying Seville oranges had to seek refuge from a storm in the harbour at Dundee. Fearing the loss of his cargo due to the delay, the shipowner put the oranges up for sale at a bargain price and they were snapped up by a local grocer, James Keiller. Some say he thought he was buying sweet oranges and was dismayed when he discovered that he had bought bitter Sevilles. Undeterred, his wife Janet added large quantities of sugar to sweeten the oranges and included the cooked peel in the finished preserve, creating marmalade as we know it today. In 1797, Keiller opened his first factory and so began Dundee's long association with marmalade.

Other companies were quick to pick up the idea of marmalade production and two leading UK brands are Frank Cooper's Oxford Marmalade and the family-owned Wilkin & Sons Tiptree Marmalade. You will find their preserves in hotels and restaurants all over the world, but their marmalade is really an integral part of an English breakfast, rounding off the best meal of the day.

Marmalade has accompanied British travellers, from explorers to travel writers and politicians, who share a reluctance to venture forth without the familiar palate-waking sweet/bitter combination of marmalade. Visit small towns, gift shops or village fetes around Britain and the chances are you will find jars of home-made marmalade on sale.

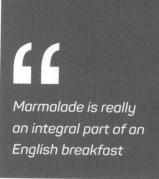

"

Marmalade is really
an integral part of an
English breakfast

ROYAL WORCESTER WEDDING MUG

When Prince Charles married Lady Diana Spencer in 1981, 600,000 people crowded the streets of London to catch a glimpse of them. Another 750 million worldwide watched their wedding on television.

Thirty years later a million people lined the route taken by Charles' son William when he married Kate Middleton and as many as two billion people worldwide were reckoned to have caught the event on TV or via the Internet. That's almost one in three people on the planet.

Royal Worcester, who made the mug shown here, dates back to 1751, making it one of the oldest remaining English pottery brands still in existence. Its 2011 royal wedding collection, 'crafted from fine bone china and finished in 22 carat gold' included a pill box, a loving cup (a cup with two handles) and a lion-head vase.

Not all the commemorative goods on sale in the run-up to the royal wedding were so concerned with maintaining dignity or respect. On offer elsewhere was Katea, teabags with pictures of the royal couple on their handles. For those disgusted by the whole event, graphic designer Lydia Leith offered a commemorative sick bag. Another company, Crown Jewels, tastefully packaged up some royal wedding condoms, and Nottingham's Castle Rock Brewery produced bottles of beer under the label 'Kiss Me Kate'.

Spare a thought, though, for the poor man who designed one royal wedding mug – the star of many news reports at the time – which included a picture of Kate Middleton together with not her husband-to-be, but her future brother-in-law, Prince Harry. We hope the maker used the publicity to sell his whole stock as a future classic.

> **For those disgusted by the whole event, graphic designer Lydia Leith offered a commemorative sick bag**

RUGBY BALL

Named after Rugby School (itself located in the town of Rugby), the traditional story is that rugby was invented in 1823 when a player named William Webb Ellis ignored the rules of football, picked up the ball and ran with it. Though the evidence for this story is weak, the international rugby governing body has named the Rugby World Cup the Webb Ellis Cup, demonstrating that one should never allow strict historical accuracy to get in the way of a good story.

Two people, Richard Lindon and William Gilbert, both boot and shoemakers and both located close to the gates of Rugby School, led the way in making the balls. Richard Lindon's wife, in addition to bearing him 17 children, also helped him make the balls, which consisted of a pig's bladder encased in leather. Her role was to blow them up using a small clay pipe and her own lung power. This proved to be very hazardous, as the pig's bladders often carried germs which could cause life-threatening diseases. It is said that Mrs Lindon herself died prematurely from such a disease.

The original pig's bladder balls tended to be plum-shaped but after 1870, with the introduction of the rubber bladder, they became more egg-shaped to aid handling. In 1892 the Rugby Football Union decided that the ball must be oval and the gradual flattening of the ball continued over the years. Despite the application of fish oil and animal fat, the leather-encased balls were prone to waterlogging, but it was not until the 1980s that leather was finally replaced by waterproof synthetics.

> *Richard Lindon's wife, in addition to bearing him 17 children, also helped him make the balls*

CHRISTMAS PUDDING

Christmas pudding is sometimes called plum pudding, even though it usually contains no plums at all. The main ingredients are flour, raisins, sultanas, currants, suet, mixed spices, dark sugars and various forms of alcohol, such as beer, brandy and rum.

Plum pudding originally contained meat (it still normally contains suet, which makes it unsuitable for vegetarians), which was stored with dry fruits to help preserve it after the autumn slaughter of livestock. As methods of preserving meat improved, however, the meat disappeared from the recipe and the fruit and sugar content increased.

The dessert can be traced back to medieval times when the Church declared that each household should prepare a pudding that included 13 ingredients, to represent Christ and the 12 apostles. It was also traditional that every member of the household should stir the pudding, making a wish at the same time. In richer households the cook would include silver coins into the pudding, making a wish at the same time. An alternative to this coin was the Christmas pudding charm. Made from silver or porcelain, you can still buy these charms today. Typically they take the form of a button, a wishbone, a bird, a coin or a horseshoe. Whoever finds the charm will be blessed with good fortune – provided of course that they have not swallowed it by mistake.

The final touch for the perfectly served Christmas pudding is to turn the lights down low and then pour brandy over it and set it alight. And as the final mouthful slips joyfully down your throat, you can start to think about your New Year's diet…

> **"**
> *Whoever finds
> the charm will
> be blessed with
> good fortune*

FISH AND CHIPS

The first fish and chip shop opened in Britain in 1860, and fish and chips quickly became the unrivalled British takeaway food – the first fast food to be offered in this country. By the 1930s, there were 35,000 fish and chip shops in the UK. Fish and chips were two of just a small number of foods not to be rationed during World War Two. It was then, and still is, a popular meal for families to have at home, or when travelling to the seaside for a day out. Today, even though the number of fish and chip shops has fallen to around 10,500 outlets, they still sell almost a quarter of all the white fish consumed in the United Kingdom, and a tenth of all the potatoes.

You do not have to go far in any British town to find one. Fish and chip shops are usually easy to spot with their brightly lit signs and a tendency (shared with British hairdressers) to come up with punning names like The Codfather, The Plaice to Be, The Frying Scotsman, Frying Nemo, A Salt N Battered, and even In Cod We Trust.

Whilst there are many places where you will be served a greasy stack of soggy battered fish on a mound of slippery soft chips, a new breed of fish and chip shops has emerged: fish and chip shops that sell high-quality fresh fish at prices which customers are willing to queue for. (One successful takeaway has even set up a webcam so that its customers can go online to check how long the queue outside their shop is.) Others have started to experiment with alternatives to the usual cod, plaice and haddock, offering more unusual seafood like calamari and mackerel, along with new flavours of batter such as massala, lemon, and lime and chilli.

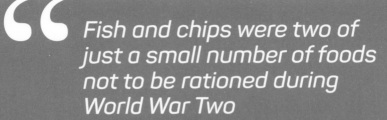

> Fish and chips were two of just a small number of foods not to be rationed during World War Two

KING JAMES BIBLE

The King James Bible – sometimes called the Authorised Version – is a book that took seven years and 47 scholars to write and has had 400 years to mature and be appreciated. Begun in 1604 and completed in 1611, it has been described as the only great work of art ever to be created by a committee.

The fact that it remains in print to this day, that it is still revered even after several attempts at creating more modern tellings of Bible stories, bears testimony to its continuing cultural significance. To understand the importance of the King James Bible you need only look at the number of phrases still in use in everyday English that come from it. Take for example: a labour of love; a bird in the hand is worth two in the bush; a leopard cannot change its spots; eat, drink and be merry; forbidden fruit; white as snow; and so on.

A 2007 survey showed that only 10 per cent of the British population attended church weekly and that two-thirds had not gone to church in the previous year. It also showed that the average age of churchgoers was increasing, suggesting that the young are not being drawn in by any of the Christian churches, including the Church of England. But in spite of the decline in church attendance the King James Bible still stands as a British icon, its poetry and language continuing to exercise an unseen and under-recognised influence.

OYSTER CARD

The Oyster card was introduced in London in 2003 and it now accounts for around 80 per cent of journeys made on London transport. To Londoners it is an everyday object, as banal as a credit card, but to anyone visiting the city for the first time – and unaccustomed to it – the Oyster card can seem part of a baffling system that sends you rushing to the nearest taxi rank.

Why is it called an Oyster card? It seems that Transport for London, who operate the system, wanted to play on the idea of the oyster as a shell that is safe and contains something valuable (the pearl being a microchip embedded inside the card). It also picks up on the saying 'the world is your oyster', in this case the key to unlocking the many hidden gems in the city.

If you plan to stay in London for more than just a few days, you will save money if you get an Oyster card. The same size as a standard credit card, the Oyster allows you to travel on London overground trains, buses and the tube at the lowest available cost. Once you have it, you will no longer have to queue to buy a ticket; you simply top it up every now and then and hold it over a card reader as you enter the train or tube station or bus.

LYLE'S GOLDEN SYRUP

In 1881, Abram Lyle set up a sugar refinery and a couple of years later noticed that the sugar cane refining process produced a treacly sort of syrup, which could be further refined. The result was a preserve and sweetener for cooking. He started selling small quantities of 'Goldie' from wooden casks to his employees and local customers. Word spread quickly, and soon Lyle was selling a tonne a week.

In 1904, the 'lion and bees' image was registered as Lyle's trademark, and it appears on the tin to this day. The design came not from an advertising agency but from Abram Lyle himself: it refers to a story in the Old Testament, in which Samson killed a lion, then saw that bees had formed a honeycomb in the lion's carcass. The words from the Bible still appear on the tin today: 'Out of the strong came forth sweetness.'

One of the marks of a successful British company has been that it becomes an official supplier to the Royal Family, an accolade that is marked by the granting of a royal warrant. Tate & Lyle gained a royal warrant for its golden syrup in 1922 and, as you might expect, it remains on the tin to this day. Even more impressive is that the company is recognised by Guinness World Records as the longest established brand in the world.

Golden syrup may be used in cooking or eaten spread on toast or crumpets. But an ideal way to sample it is by ordering one of the most popular desserts on British pub menus: treacle pudding – with custard, of course.

Out of the strong came forth sweetness

RAILWAY STATION SIGN

If you want to find your way to the railway station in any town or city in Britain, then look out for the symbol shown here, two opposite-facing arrows set on two parallel lines.

This design was created in 1965 as a logo for British Rail, the nationalised rail system at that time. Even though British Rail was broken up in the 1990s and is now operated by a number of separate companies, the logo remains. One reason for its continued use is that it is a simple and elegant representation of the railway system – the parallel lines evoking the railway tracks and the two interlocking arrows representing trains passing one another, one heading east, the other west.

The design was created by Gerald Burney, who worked for a consultancy called the Design Research Unit and his graphic has outlived the early criticism it received.

The British railway system has been the butt of many jokes over the years, gaining a reputation for late trains and dry, taste-free sandwiches. So it is maybe not so surprising that Burney's new design came in for its own share of criticism. Some commentators complained about the loss of the lion crest on the previous British Railways flag, while others contemptuously compared the design to a piece of barbed wire. But the fact is that the symbol has survived, even though the unloved organisation it represented has long gone. A tribute to the effectiveness of this deceptively simple design.

Goostrey

> " Others contemptuously compared the design to a piece of barbed wire

TARTAN KILT

The kilt is a knee-length, skirt-like garment, with pleats at the back, mostly associated today with Scotland, with variants found in other Celtic countries including Wales and Ireland. It has no pockets so it is typically worn with a sporran, a pouch which hangs at the front of the kilt. It dates back at least to the sixteenth century and the word may derive from the Old Norse *kjalta*. As for the tartan, the earliest example in Scotland dates from the third century AD – found stuffed into the top of a pot containing Roman coins.

The tartan kilt is – along with bagpipes – the most visible physical symbol of Scottish identity. In the past that strong association has led to it being banned, because of fears held by King George II of the threat posed by warrior Highland clans. In 1746 a 'Dress Act' was passed banning kilts, with severe penalties for those breaking the law. That ban lasted 35 years, but when King

George IV visited Scotland in 1822, himself wearing a kilt, the fashion for kilt-wearing, which continues to this day, was firmly established.

Today the kilt is generally only worn on special occasions – celebrations like weddings, Hogmanay (the welcoming of the New Year) or a *ceilidh* (a traditional dance with folk music). A good kilt, together with the accompanying jacket, sporran, hose, brogues and accessories can cost you over £1,000, but with care can last a lifetime.

RED NOSE

In 1988, the first Comic Relief Red Nose Day, a charity fundraising event, was held, and has taken place every two years ever since. The charity Comic Relief was formed in 1985 and initially consisted of one-off TV programmes and appeals. It was the creation of Red Nose Day that really put it on the map, bringing together sponsorship money, fundraising activities by members of the public and straight donations to the charity. All of this is focused on a single all-evening TV programme hosted by the BBC in March each second year.

The Comic Relief red nose is given away in exchange for a donation and has taken on many forms over the years. Initially it was simply a shiny red hollow plastic sphere with a slit at the back to fit over your nose. In 1991 it grew a couple of small arms and in 1995 it was heat-sensitive, changing colour with

the temperature. It has continued to evolve, having gone fluffy and having gained various faces. The 2003 nose featured spikey hair, which, when worn upside down, looked like a moustache.

In 2011, the red nose was one of the three distinct monster noses shown here: Captain Conk with a pirate's eyepatch and skull and crossbones scarf; Honkus with a broad mouth and piranha-like teeth; and finally the more nerdy Chucklechomp, wearing glasses.

Over the years tens of millions of noses have been sold, contributing to the mind-boggling sums raised by Comic Relief for charities all over the world.

PUB SIGN

The pub (short for public house) remains the social centre of many communities in Britain. The oldest pub today, according to Guinness World Records, is Ye Olde Fighting Cocks in St Albans, which can trace its history back almost a thousand years. Since 1393, all pubs have been obliged by law to carry a pub sign: 'Whosoever shall brew ale in the town with intention of selling it must hang out a sign, otherwise he shall forfeit his ale.'

Pubs have often changed their names to pick up on events like battles or military leaders (The Lord Nelson) or local activities such as trades (The Bricklayers' Arms) or sports (The Cricketers' Arms) or after the reigning monarch (the pub in the BBC soap opera EastEnders is the Queen Victoria, known to its patrons as The Queen Vic). Some reflect their times – The Coach & Horses would probably date from the eighteenth century and be on one of the early highways, while

The Railway Inn would have been built a century or more later.

There is a story that, in Stony Stratford, midway on the journey between London and the Midlands, the London coach would change horses at a pub named The Bull, and the Birmingham coach across the road would stop at The Cock Inn. The passengers from each coach would swap news while waiting for the change, and it is from this that the phrase 'cock and bull story' (meaning a ridiculous and unbelievable story) is said to have originated.

The pub continues to evolve so, though their numbers may continue to fall, they will certainly not disappear.

> **Since 1393, all pubs have been obliged by law to carry a pub sign**

BOTTLE OF BITTER & TWISTED BEER

Old Thumper, Hobgoblin, Fursty Ferret, Waggle Dance, Bruins Ruin, Piddle in the Hole: just some of the strange and playful names of beers that you can find on any supermarket shelf in Britain.

The beer bottle shown here is Harviestoun Brewery's award-winning Bitter & Twisted. This Scottish brewery was started in 1984 by Ken Brooker, who had previously worked for the Ford Motor Company for over 20 years. The beer was named by Ken's wife as a humorous reference to him. One of their other beers is a dark stout (also shown here), which Ken named Old Engine Oil, as its colour reminded him of the black oil drained from the sump of a car.

Together with a friend, Ken started the brewery on a farm in Scotland, and in 2007 their efforts were rewarded when Bitter & Twisted was named 'World's Best Ale' at the World Beer Awards.

The 1960s and 1970s probably saw the low point for British beer drinkers, as the choice of beers available to them shrunk. Taste was sacrificed in favour of convenience. British beer drinkers of a certain age will remember with horror the fizzy, characterless beers like Double Diamond and Watneys Red Barrel, which were once the only beers on tap in many British pubs. Out of this drought of good beer emerged a movement – The Campaign for Real Ale (CAMRA) – whose aim was to preserve traditional 'real' beer-making. Forty years later the organisation still thrives, with many thousands of members and its own annual *Good Beer Guide*, which features pubs serving the UK's most 'interesting' beers.

British beer drinkers of a certain age will remember with horror the fizzy, characterless beers like Double Diamond and Watneys Red Barrel

EDDIE STOBART LORRY

Eddie Stobart is a transport company that has operated large lorries up and down Britain for over 40 years. It is now so large that it claims its vehicles cover the equivalent of 24 laps of the earth every day and that it makes a delivery in Europe every 20 seconds. A remarkable commercial success, but otherwise you might say: nothing unusual.

What is remarkable about Eddie Stobart is that over that time it has captured the imagination of the British public so strongly that it now has its own fan club, which people pay to join. It sells models of its vehicles, has its own range of cartoon characters and has even inspired a song by The Wurzels: 'I Want to Be an Eddie Stobart Driver'.

Quite how Eddie Stobart came to gain such a unique place in popular British culture is unclear. Perhaps it has something to do with the unusual, but friendly, name, which is written in large, clear script on the side of all its vehicles. Perhaps it is also reinforced by the consistent green, red and white colour scheme on its lorries, which from the start 'Steady' Eddie Stobart insisted should be kept smart and clean. Eddie also required his drivers to wear shirts and ties.

Or perhaps Eddie Stobart's popularity is connected to the way the firm gives all its lorries names – mostly female ones, the originals being Twiggy, Dolly, Tammy and Suzi. This has encouraged an army of spotters – presumably bored on long motorway journeys – to record their sightings of the firm's lorries. Members of the fan club can even ask to name a lorry, but in case you are tempted to apply you should note that there is a three-year waiting list.

" I Want to Be an Eddie Stobart Driver

PORK PIE

The pork pie is a traditional English meat pie, made with seasoned chopped pork, sealed in a thin coating of jelly and wrapped in a pastry case. Eat it cold or, if you are lucky, warm, fresh from the oven; eat it on its own, or with brown sauce, pickles or salad.

The best known is the Melton Mowbray pork pie, which has recently been granted Protected Geographical Indication (PGI) status by the EU. If it says Melton Mowbray on the label then the pie will have been made by one of just ten licensed producers from the region around Melton Mowbray in Leicestershire. It will have been made using fresh, chopped (not minced) pork and will look grey, not pink like pork pies made from cured pork.

Many people in England take their pork pies very seriously. The Pork Pie Appreciation Society, started in 1982 by some less-than-dedicated fitness enthusiasts, meets weekly at the Old Bridge Inn at Ripponden in Yorkshire. Each week its members bring along pies, rating them out of ten for taste, texture and general appeal.

And for those further afield the forum on the Society's website caters for any questions members may have about pork pies, such as 'How can an expat living in New Mexico get his hands on a decent pork pie?' Answer: 'Contact the English Pork Pie Company in New York (whose owners used to make pork pies in Yorkshire) and get them to ship some freshly baked ones out by FedEx.'

REMEMBRANCE POPPY

The remembrance poppy consists of a green plastic stem with a single green paper leaf, a red petal cluster and a black centre. It appears each year as part of the Royal British Legion's Poppy Appeal. In this simple form the poppy is unpretentious. It is, after all, not the object, but the sentiment behind it that counts. You can, if you want, buy more expensive poppies: for example a poppy brooch encrusted with Swarovski crystals was auctioned in 2007 for almost £2,850, but such poppies are unusual.

The remembrance poppy appears in autumn every year, usually sold from small counter-top display units in shops, clubs and pubs, and in the street by volunteers. Poppies are worn on Remembrance Day, 11 November each year, and on Remembrance Sunday, the Sunday nearest to 11 November

each year, which honour those who gave their lives fighting in wars, and in World War One in particular. The money raised – nearly £40 million each year – is used to improve the lives of conflict survivors, many of whom have to cope with severe injuries.

Why red poppies? Apart from the obvious significance of red as a symbol of blood shed by soldiers, they are mentioned in the famous poem 'In Flanders fields', written during World War One by a Canadian officer called John McRae, who was inspired by the resilience of the red poppies that continued to grow – against all odds – in the battlefields of Belgium:

In Flanders fields
the poppies blow
Between the crosses,
row on row.

MANCHESTER UNITED FOOTBALL SHIRT

For many football-loving children in Manchester – and all over the world, for that matter – there is only one shirt they want to wear: Manchester United.

Things did not start well for the club, though. Formed by the Lancashire and Yorkshire Railway in 1878 as Newton Heath LYR Football Club, it joined the new Football League in its top Division, but after two seasons was relegated to the Second Division. Worse was to come. By 1902, it was on the brink of bankruptcy and had to be rescued by local businessmen. They renamed the club Manchester United.

The club's fortunes between the two world wars went up and then down, with relegation followed by promotion and relegation once more, but after World War Two, under legendary manager Matt Busby, the club achieved more consistent success.

In 1968, Busby and his team won the European Cup, the first English team to do so. That team included legendary players such as Bobby Charlton, Denis Law and George Best. From 1969, when Busby retired, the club went through a number of managers before Sir Alex Ferguson joined in 1986. Like Busby, Ferguson changed the club's fortunes and in 1999 they won the Premier League, the FA Cup and the UEFA Champions League in the same season – the first English club to achieve this feat.

Like Ferrari in motor racing, Manchester United remains appealing precisely because it has had its ups and downs over many years. And that is why small boys all over the world will continue to badger their parents with demands for the latest shirt design, bearing the ever-changing names of its sponsors.

HAGGIS

Haggis tastes better than you dare to expect. Knowing that it is made of a sheep's heart, liver and lungs minced with onion, oatmeal and suet, and cooked in an animal's intestine for three hours does not at first sound promising. But the reality can be surprisingly good: a sausage or pudding with a nutty texture and a pleasing savoury taste.

Haggis is the traditional Scottish dish, its status confirmed by the country's foremost poet, Robert Burns, in his poem 'Address to a Haggis', written in 1787. In the opening stanza Burns personifies the food:

Fair fa' your honest, sonsie face,
Great chieftain o' the puddin' race!
Aboon them a' ye tak your place,
Painch, tripe, or thairm:
Weel are ye worthy o' a grace
As lang's my arm.

All over Scotland, and in any part of the world where Scots now live, Burns Night (25 January, the poet's birthday) is the night on which to eat haggis, served with neeps (swede) and tatties (potatoes) and washed down with a dram of Scotch whisky (see p.90).

*Fair fa' your honest,
sonsie face*

CHRISTMAS CRACKER

The Christmas cracker is a vital part of the traditional British Christmas dinner. Family members – children, parents, grandparents, aunts and uncles, cousins and friends – pull crackers with one another at the start of the meal and will then be seen, young and old, wearing the coloured paper hats taken from inside them.

The Christmas cracker was invented by a London baker and confectioner called Thomas J. Smith in the 1840s. Sales of his wrapped bon-bon sweets had been disappointing so he decided to make them more appealing by adding mottos inside the twisted paper wrapping, rather in the style of the fortune cookie. But it was only when he added the cracker – a small explosion generated by chemicals on two paper strips, set off by friction – that sales started to grow.

Smith had to make the wrapper bigger to accommodate the cracker mechanism, and in due course the sweet was replaced by a small gift. The paper party hat followed. The gift will vary in quality depending on the price paid for the cracker, but might be anything from a plastic paper clip, puzzle, small screwdriver or key ring to a pair of nail clippers.

An important element in the contemporary cracker is the inclusion of a joke (or sometimes a motto or riddle) and the joke is invariably very bad, such as:

Question: What do you call a blind reindeer? Answer: No eye deer.

Some claim that the jokes are deliberately terrible so that this puts less pressure on the person reading it out. After all, if the joke is known to be weak then no one can blame the teller for failing to do it justice.

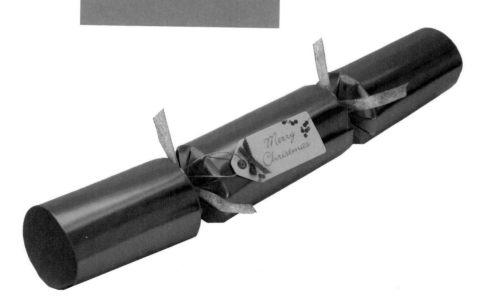

SCHOOL UNIFORM

The earliest records of school uniforms in Britain date back to the sixteenth century. So-called Bluecoat schools required their schoolboys and apprentices to wear long blue coats – blue being favoured because it was a cheap dye, and so was affordable, as well as suggesting humility. Christ's Hospital School in Sussex retains a form of this coat as part of its uniform to this day.

The uniform shown here is that worn by students at Stockport Grammar School, whose history dates back to 1487, when it was founded through a legacy bequeathed by Sir Edmund Shaa – a former mayor of London. Most schools in Britain, including those with much shorter history, require a uniform, usually consisting of at least a blazer or sweater in school colours, together with a dark skirt or trousers.

For centuries education in Britain was the preserve of the rich or of the beneficiaries of charity, attending schools that were often controlled by the Church. It was not until 1870 that the Elementary Education Act introduced free primary education for all children up to the age of 12 and most of the new schools founded at that time required a uniform.

Many schools have now acted to simplify or modernise their uniforms, for example by allowing boys to dispense with ties and blazers and letting girls wear trousers. For the moment, though, there is no sign of any move to change national policy on school uniforms, as all the major political parties are still in favour of them.

> "So-called Bluecoat schools required their schoolboys and apprentices to wear long blue coats"

RED DOUBLE-DECKER BUS

What do a Ferrari and a double-decker bus have in common? The answer (apart from the obvious one that they both have an engine and wheels) is that they look best in bright scarlet red. Double-deckers exist all over the world, but the red double-decker bus is instantly associated with Britain in general, and with London in particular.

The red London bus even inspired its own song, written and performed by the duo Flanders & Swann, entitled 'A Transport of Delight', which sings the praises of the 97 horse-power omnibus.

The best known London bus is the Routemaster, introduced in 1956, which saw active service in London for almost 50 years (and you will still see some refurbished ones on the streets of London today, mostly on heritage and tourist routes). Many of them covered millions of miles before being refurbished and sold abroad. When they were phased out from general use in 2005 there was some outcry because they were replaced by the longer and more cumbersome bendy bus.

Now, however, they have been replaced by the twenty-first-century New Routemaster, shown here. Designed by (Thomas) Heatherwick Studio and built by Wrightbus in Ballymena in Northern Ireland, the new bus includes the same hop-on, hop-off platform as the original, but naturally uses new more energy-efficient technology.

" A Transport of Delight "

WELLINGTON BOOTS

The wellington boot, often known as a 'welly' or gumboot, was originally made of leather and popularised by the famous British military leader, Arthur Wellesley, 1st Duke of Wellington. Later known as the Iron Duke, Wellington became a British hero after he defeated Napoleon at the Battle of Waterloo in 1815.

Wellington wanted a boot that would be hard-wearing for battle, yet comfortable if worn in the evening, and he instructed his shoemaker, Hoby of St James's Street in London, to create a long tight-fitting boot that would meet his requirements. Wellington boots quickly caught on with patriotic British gentlemen eager to copy their war hero.

The best-known British brand of wellington boot is Hunter, which was started in the late nineteenth century when an American gentleman called Mr Henry Lee Norris moved from the United States to Scotland and set up a new factory making wellington boots not from leather, but from rubber.

In 1955 Hunter introduced the green welly, which came to be identified with a particular kind of person who would spend the weekends in the country and the week in the city. Such people quickly became known as the 'green welly brigade'.

In 1976, having supplied wellingtons to the royal households, Hunter was awarded a royal warrant. Since then Hunter boots have become an essential fashion item that is more often associated with music festivals like Glastonbury than any more hazardous pursuit.

"

Wellington wanted a boot that would be hard-wearing for battle, yet comfortable if worn in the evening

IRN-BRU

Irn-Bru is a fizzy non-alcoholic drink produced in Scotland, and its unusual name and quirky advertising over many years has given it a distinctively Scottish character. You can buy it throughout the United Kingdom, and elsewhere in the world, for that matter – anywhere where there is a large community of people from its native Scotland. Known for its bright orange colour and sweet, slightly citrus flavour, the Irn-Bru recipe, like that of Coca-Cola, is a closely guarded secret.

Originally called 'Iron Brew', it is thought that the name originated when Glasgow Central Station was being rebuilt in 1901. To discourage workers from the William Beardmore and Company Steel Works in Glasgow from quenching their thirst with large quantities of beer (and so becoming incapable of working properly) a non-alcoholic source of refreshment was sought. Local drinks manufacturer, A. G. Barr,

offered a soft drink and the name arose because of its connections to the steel and iron works.

In 1946, a change in the law required A. G. Barr to update the name as the drink is not actually brewed. That was when the phonetic spelling was substituted, Irn-Bru, mimicking the pronunciation in a Glasgow accent.

Advertisements for Irn-Bru have sometimes been controversial, drawing complaints from the public. For example, one campaign featured a young woman in a bikini, accompanied by the slogan 'I never knew four and a half inches could give me so much pleasure' (four and a half inches being the height of the canned version of the drink), while yet another had a black and white picture of a well-dressed but stuffy-looking older man saying 'I don't like Irn-Bru but I'm just a silly old banker'. As far as we know there were no complaints about this ad.

I never knew four and a half inches could give me so much pleasure

DR. MARTENS BOOTS

The first Dr. Martens boot made by the Griggs family at their Rushden factory in Northamptonshire in 1960 was almost identical to the one shown here. The original concept was to create a working boot using an air-cushioned sole to aid comfort.

Credit for the design goes to the original Doctor Märtens, a German who invented them when he hurt his ankle in a skiing accident. The British company Griggs, which took up the licence to make them, was at first glance an unlikely licensee, being a traditional British shoe manufacturer, more associated with hand-made shoes for the gentry. But the boot, marketed under the brand name Airwair, achieved rapid success in a new market that Griggs had not attracted up to then – the working class.

In the 1970s, they were adopted by skinheads, some of whom would expose the steel toecaps of their boots to make them more intimidating, and later they were taken up by punks. And all the while they continued to be popular with policemen, many of whom would be confronting protestors and angry young men, many wearing Doc Martens themselves.

For a while after 2003 production of Doc Martens stopped in Britain and was moved to China and Thailand but in 2007 it came back. In 2010, a Doc Martens boot won two fashion awards at the 2010 Fashion Show in New York City; one for the 'most popular men's footwear in latest fashion' and the other for 'best counter-cultural footwear of the decade'.

How many other products appeal so powerfully to both lawmakers and lawbreakers, to free-thinkers and to the establishment?

*The original concept
was to create a
working boot using
an air-cushioned
sole to aid comfort*

BOTTLE OF SCOTCH WHISKY

Whisky has been produced in Scotland for centuries, possibly for a thousand years (the earliest written record goes back to the fifteenth century). A word of warning here: Scotch whisky should not be confused with whiskey with an 'e', which typically refers to Irish or American alternatives. To indicate just how significant a part whisky plays in Scottish culture, the word whisky itself comes from the Gaelic *usquebaugh*, which means 'water of life'.

If you want to appreciate Scotch whisky better, but without travelling round all the distilleries, you could order a 'Scotch whisky aroma nosing kit', which will give you up to 24 samples of Scotch whisky 'aromas' covering the spectrum typically found in Scotch whiskies, together with a guide book. By this means you will be able to impress your friends by talking convincingly about the best 'nosing action' and overwhelm them with your knowledge of the little-known hazard of 'tired nose syndrome'.

Most of the Scotch whisky that you will find both in Scotland and in bars around the world is blended – in other words it has been created by combining whiskies produced by a number of different distilleries. Typical brands are Bell's, Dewar's and Johnnie Walker.

For real Scotch whisky aficionados, there is nothing to compare with a fine single malt whisky, such as the 21-year-old single malt pictured here, from Old Pulteney Distillery in Wick – made using malted barley at a single distillery and then matured for at least three years in oak casks previously used for bourbon or sherry. The finest of malt whiskies have been matured for 40 years or more and are, not surprisingly, very expensive.

CORNISH PASTY

Since 2011, the Cornish pasty has enjoyed Protected Geographical Indication (PGI) status under EU law. This means that a genuine Cornish pasty now has to be made in Cornwall, must have the distinctive D-shaped pastry case – crimped at the side rather than at the top – and must contain chunks of beef, potato, swede (but never carrot) and onion. Seasoning is added, but no artificial flavourings or preservatives, and then it must be baked slowly.

For hundreds of years Cornish working people had eaten pasties; it was the traditional Cornishman's packed lunch, easy to make and easy to eat (whether out on Bodmin Moor or down a tin mine), and today it offers the same advantages.

Some have suggested that Cornish pasties were side-crimped so that miners could eat while holding them by their thick edge. They would then throw the crust away after eating the rest, in that way avoiding contact between dirty fingers and food. This seems unlikely, however, given that the miners were not well off and would scarcely have thrown away good food. In addition, there are photos showing people eating pasties wrapped in paper or muslin; a much simpler and less wasteful solution.

'Oggy' is a slang term for a Cornish pasty, derived from its Cornish name of 'hoggan'. Legend has it that tin-miners' wives, or pasty bakers, would shout 'oggy, oggy, oggy' to announce that pasties were ready, with the miners responding 'oi! oi! oi!' in acknowledgment. More recently, this has been adopted as a popular rugby chant.

WELSH LAVERBREAD

Laver is an edible seaweed that grows along the coastlines of the Irish Sea, around the western shores of Britain and down the east side of Ireland. It is used for making laverbread – a traditional Welsh delicacy, known locally there as 'bara lawr' and referred to by some as 'Welshman's caviar'.

Although the laver grows plentifully along the coastlines around the Irish Sea, it is laborious to pick. There is no way of automating the process, so it has to be gathered by hand. Once picked the laver must be rinsed thoroughly, before being boiled and then minced, to create a paste-like texture. And this process gives it another similarity to caviar – it tends to be expensive.

At first sight, when you open a pack of laverbread it can be a little off-putting, as you are faced with a dark, slightly sinister-looking,

slimy gunge. But do not be put off. If you are used to eating, say, cooked spinach and you like seafood, then laverbread should hold no fears. A quick taste of the raw paste reveals a sea-salty flavour tinged with the same iron tang that you get with cooked spinach or spring greens. And laverbread is highly nutritious, rich in protein along with important minerals iron and iodine, and containing vitamins A, B, B2, C and D. It is also very low in calories.

DYSON VACUUM CLEANER

The vacuum cleaner first became common in British homes around the 1960s and the leading brand at that time was Hoover. So widespread was its use that many British people still use the word Hoover to describe any vacuum cleaner, regardless of the actual brand. Today, however, it is Dyson, rather than Hoover, that sells the greatest number of vacuum cleaners in the UK.

If James Dyson were American he would probably be admired as the embodiment of the American dream: a man who passionately believed in making things better, who got into debt in pursuit of his dream and who, most importantly of all, succeeded in his quest and became one of the richest men in the country.

Dyson's first successful product was a wheelbarrow that used a plastic ball instead of a wheel, which he called the Ballbarrow.

But it was when, in the 1970s, he turned his attention to the vacuum cleaner that he really hit the jackpot. Noticing that traditional vacuum cleaners, which use bags to catch the dust, lost efficiency very quickly, he set about developing a new kind of cleaner, using the cyclonic separation principle that would do away with bags altogether.

When other manufacturers turned him away Dyson was undeterred and set up his own manufacturing company. He claims it took him 'fifteen years of frustration, perseverance, and over 5,000 prototypes' to launch the Dyson DC01 vacuum cleaner under his own name. Within 22 months it became the best-selling cleaner in the UK. 'I wanted to give up almost every day... A lot of people give up when the world seems to be against them, but that's the point when you should push a little harder.'

" *Fifteen years of frustration, perseverance, and over 5,000 prototypes* **"**

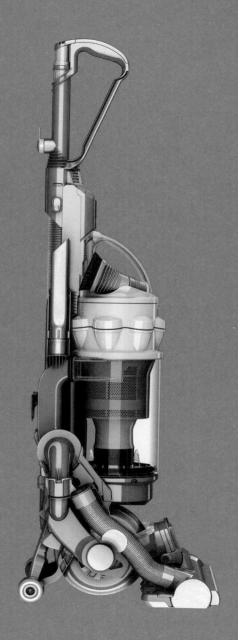

AGA COOKER

It was the Nobel-prize-winning Swedish physicist Gustaf Dalén who invented the heat storage cooker in 1922. At the time, he was working for a Swedish company, AGA, and had been blinded by an explosion at work. While recuperating at home Dalén came up with the idea for a new kind of cooker, which would save his wife the need to keep relighting her solid-fuel stove.

In Britain there is another company, independent from the Swedish AGA, called AGA Rangemaster. The latter took out a licence from the Swedish company in 1929, and has carried on making the world-famous AGA, and later also Rayburn heat storage cookers, ever since.

Because the AGA is on all the time and remains constantly hot there is no need to keep switching it on and off, making it convenient to use, and it keeps the kitchen snug and welcoming in a chilly British winter. This of course can become a drawback in summer.

The AGA is most at home in the generously sized kitchen of a large Victorian house, a converted barn or country farmhouse. It has also become associated with a certain kind of novel, known as the 'AGA saga', popularised in the 1990s by the novelist Joanna Trollope and which typically featured well-off middle-class women living in country villages in the south of England.

> **Dalén came up with the idea for a new kind of cooker, which would save his wife the need to keep relighting her solid-fuel stove**

TESCO CARRIER BAG

In Hollywood movies, the hero or heroine emerging from their local grocery store will typically be clutching a brown paper bag stuffed with their purchases. In Britain, it would be a plastic bag branded with the name of one of the country's leading supermarkets – Tesco, Sainsbury's, Waitrose, ASDA or Morrisons. We get through billions of plastic bags each year and around two million of those bear the red-and-blue Tesco logo. Such is Tesco's presence in the UK that it accounts for around one pound in every ten spent by British consumers, and so it is not surprising that it gets through more bags than its competitors too.

But consumers are increasingly being encouraged to buy and use reusable bags, to reduce plastic consumption, waste and pollution. Since October 2011, Welsh retailers have been obliged by law to charge five pence for each carrier bag used by customers, an initiative that has since been followed in Northern Ireland, Scotland and England, resulting in a substantial reduction in the number of bags used in all four nations.

THREE-PIN PLUG

The standard British plug is distinctive but not very elegant. With its large body and long squared-off pins, it looks like a dead, overweight three-legged beetle.

The original design was created 70 years ago, and until recently no effort has been put into revising it, probably because no one saw any pressing need to do so. Concerned that the previous two-pin system could be dangerous, a government-appointed committee came up with the three-pin solution just after World War Two. The third pin that they specified is a safety earth that prevents access to the live connections, for example if a small child tries to push its fingers into the socket.

Min-Kyu Choi, a graduate of the Royal College of Art, designed a collapsible version (the 'Mu') that reduces the thickness of the plug to that of an Apple MacBook Air. By allowing the two live pins to turn though 90 degrees, he created a plug that will fit into existing wall sockets, but which can also quickly and effectively be folded away flat for storage in a laptop bag.

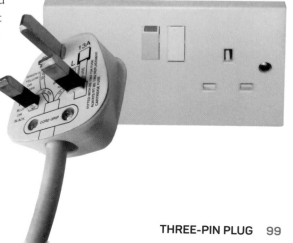

HUNTING PINK

'Hunting pink' is the term used to describe the traditional clothing worn by those who hunt in Britain. And you may well wonder why it is called 'pink' when it is so obviously bright red. The usual explanation is that it was named after one Thomas Pink, a tailor who made hunting jackets (although the brand is now more famous for its shirts). But it seems that the hunting outfit was already being called pink some time before Pink the tailor came on the scene.

Another suggestion is that in the past pink was often used to mean 'excellent' (just as today someone might say they are 'in the pink', meaning that they feel very well), but again there is no obvious link to hunting.

Hunting has its supporters in Britain, but there has also been a long tradition of hunt protesters objecting to what they see as the cruelty of fox hunting in particular.

Their campaigns to disrupt hunts by laying false trails or getting in the way of the horses led to legislation that has rendered hunting illegal in Scotland, England and Wales.

Hunts do continue to take place as The Hunting Act 2004 (applicable in England and Wales) only stops hunting where an animal is being chased; it does not stop 'drag hunting' – where dogs are trained to follow an artificial scent. Traditionally hunting has always been viewed as an upper-class pastime, and though there is some evidence that its appeal is now widening, it still remains very much a minority sport.

> ❝
> *In the past pink
> was often used to
> mean 'excellent'*

GARDEN SHED

A shed is usually a simple, single-storey structure in a back garden or on an allotment which is generally used for storage, for practising hobbies or as a workshop. Of course, sheds exist all over the world, but in Britain the shed has particular cultural significance. It is where British people, especially men, retreat to, in order to 'potter'; to 'escape'; to 'do stuff'.

It is their refuge from the rest of the world, a place where they can dismantle a motorbike without having to suffer the abuse they might otherwise earn if they carried out the same task on the kitchen table. In exceptional circumstances the shed may also be used to sleep in, say, if their owners have locked themselves out of their homes after a night at the pub. And whilst it may still be men who most often seek refuge in their shed, increasingly women are also enjoying their own space there.

The typical British garden shed is small – as little as three or four square metres of floor space – and made of wood, usually with at least one window. Gardeners use theirs as a potting shed, whilst hobbyists pursue their favoured leisure interests, which could include activities such as woodturning, pottery, painting, or laying out model railways.

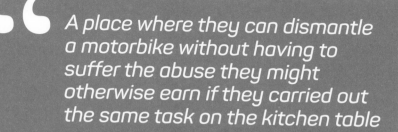

"A place where they can dismantle a motorbike without having to suffer the abuse they might otherwise earn if they carried out the same task on the kitchen table

YORKSHIRE PUDDING

The Yorkshire pudding is a key ingredient in the traditional British Sunday dinner, which consists of roasted meat, roast potatoes, vegetables, gravy and... Yorkshire pudding. The meat is normally beef, a meat so much part of British history that the French at one time called British people *les rosbifs* (the roast beefs) – perhaps one of the more complimentary things that the French have thought to call their British neighbours over the centuries. Yorkshire pudding is not just served with beef, though; it can also accompany other meats such as pork, lamb or chicken, or vegetarian options such as nut roast.

The Yorkshire pudding is made with milk, flour and eggs – similar to the mixture used to make pancakes – and rises during cooking. It can either be made as a single large dish, which is then cut up before serving, or as smaller individual puddings like the one pictured here.

No one is entirely sure how or why the Yorkshire pudding originally came about. It could have been chosen as a way of using up the fat that would drip from meat when it was cooked, but perhaps more importantly in poorer households it would be served as a separate dish, before the more expensive meat dish, intended as a way of reducing the appetite. A variant of the Yorkshire pudding is toad-in-the-hole, which is a Yorkshire pudding with sausages baked into it – served as a dish in its own right.

DIGESTIVE BISCUIT

The British are reported to be the biggest biscuit eaters in the world – and at the top of the British biscuit tree sits the 'digestive': hard, crisp, crumbly and (with a little bit of skill) good for dunking in your cup of tea. And there, of course, lies the secret of the biscuit. It is the perfect match for the British tea break.

Some claim that the term 'digestive' is derived from the belief that these biscuits had antacid properties, due to the use of sodium bicarbonate when they were first developed in the late nineteenth century. However, there are references to digestive biscuits in earlier recipe books, such as the one in *The Royal English and Foreign Confectioner* (1862) which contained just brown flour, salt, a little butter and water. It is unlikely that this recipe would ever have become Britain's favourite biscuit, unlike the current digestive, which is a development of recipes created in the nineteenth century by Huntley & Palmers and McVitie's.

Digestive biscuits are popular in food preparation for making into bases for cheesecakes and banoffee pie. Chocolate digestive biscuits, more recently coated on one side with milk, dark or white chocolate (plus orange and caramel variants), were originally produced by McVitie's in 1925 as the simple Homewheat Chocolate Digestive. American travel writer Bill Bryson has described the chocolate digestive as 'a British masterpiece'.

TEAPOT

Tea remains the archetypal British hot drink, whether it is the traditional English Breakfast tea or other varieties which have become increasingly popular, such as Earl Grey or green tea, or caffeine-free options like rooibos, fruit teas and herbal teas.

British society started to become less formal from the 1960s on, and the formality of making tea in a pot has largely been replaced by the adoption of an American invention: the tea bag. Today more than 90 per cent of tea sold in Britain is in that form and most tea is now made in a cup or mug, without the need for the teapot.

In spite of the decline in teapot usage, many contemporary designers continue to play with teapot design and decoration. Designers like Cath Kidston, who makes teapots in distinctive pastel colours, and Emma Bridgewater, whose polka dot teapot is shown

here, continue to develop teapot designs in keeping with current customer tastes.

Then there is a wholly different category of teapot owner: the collector. For such people it is not the function but the form of the teapot that counts, and the more extraordinary the better.

The Teapottery in Yorkshire caters for just this market, continuing a '200-year-old tradition of making eccentric, novelty teapots in fine English ceramics'. Each teapot is cast and decorated by hand and the company specialises in creating teapots in the form of pretty much anything you care to ask for: a caravan, a cake, a cocktail bar, a tent, a wash basin, an espresso machine, a piano (as shown here), or even a replica of the front door of 10 Downing Street.

It is not the function but the form of the teapot that counts

ORDNANCE SURVEY MAP

The Ordnance Survey map – with its distinctive contour lines showing height above sea level – has played a major part in encouraging one of the great British pastimes: walking.

It has survived the invention of the satnav because many love its facility not just to plan a route, but also to catch other features of interest along the way. Where many satnavs have left lorries stranded on narrow tracks, too tight for them to pass through, no Ordnance Survey map ever so badly misled its user.

The first moves to carry out comprehensive and accurate mapping of Britain date back to early in the eighteenth century, but it was only in 1791 that fears of an invasion by the French provided the motivation to get systematic mapping work underway.

At that time the Ministry of Defence was known as the Board of Ordnance, which is where the unusual name for the maps came from. Naturally, as the threat from the French was focused on the south-east of England, that was the first area to be mapped. As it happened, the French never did invade, but by then the advantages of mapping the country had been recognised. Over the following years the whole of the United Kingdom was surveyed and recorded.

OS maps are not just for walking, or even for cycling or keeping in the car. They are for looking at, for enjoying. Each is a highly resolved work of art, craft, design and cartography. A single map can keep you engrossed for hours on a rainy day, as you discover features of the landscape or intriguing roads and paths that bring out the explorer in you. They are, in short, masterpieces of clear, functional and remarkably beautiful design.

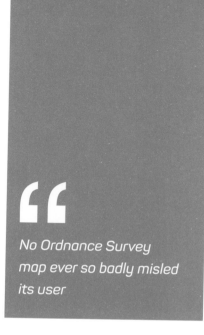

"

No Ordnance Survey
map ever so badly misled
its user

FLORAL WALLPAPER

The British have a bit of a love affair with flowers on wallpaper – and on fabrics as well, come to that. In 1996 IKEA even ran an advertising campaign encouraging British consumers to get rid of all their old floral-patterned furniture, telling them to 'chuck out the chintz!' They were encouraged to embrace IKEA's own simpler Scandinavian aesthetic instead. The campaign was a very successful one and IKEA has been just as successful in the UK as it has been around the world.

Yet so strong is the British love of flowers and floral designs that they have never been persuaded to abandon them completely. The granddaddy of them all is probably Sanderson, which can trace its history back to 1860 when Arthur Sanderson started importing French wallpapers. The firm went on over the next 150 years to commission major artists and designers like Pablo Picasso, John Piper and Lucienne Day to create their designs. In the 1970s the company promoted a co-ordinated approach to interior decor by creating floral designs that enabled householders to use the same fabric for wallcoverings, curtains and soft furnishings, accompanied by the strapline 'Very Sanderson'.

The greatest of all the exponents of floral wallpaper design, though, was the nineteenth-century designer William Morris, who was also a philosopher, scholar and writer. As the founder of the Arts and Crafts movement Morris created a distinctive 'look' featuring intricate flowing patterns of intertwined stems, leaves and flowers, which influenced many designers who followed him. His work is continued today by the company Morris & Co., whose designs can be found on wallpapers, furnishings, bags and even umbrellas.

Morris created a distinctive 'look' featuring intricate flowing patterns of intertwined stems, leaves and flowers

TWEED JACKET

The tweed jacket can be very versatile. As part of a beautifully tailored three-piece Savile Row woollen suit, tweed is the epitome of Britishness, or at least of a certain kind of Britishness. At the opposite end of the fashion scale, tweed becomes an old jacket in traditionally earthy shades of brown and green, perhaps with leather elbow patches – the wear of choice for your favourite old schoolteacher.

Tweed is hard-wearing, sometimes a little rough to the touch, but always aristocratically elegant. With a lighter-weight cloth and some design flair it can also be stylish, and even at home on the catwalks, bearing designer labels like Westwood and Galliano.

The original name of tweed was *tweel*, or *twill*, and according to folklore, became tweed only when the word *tweels* on a letter sent by a Scottish firm to a London merchant was misread as tweed, the name of a river that flows through the area close to the Scottish border. The name stuck.

Tweed comes from Scotland, with the best known being Harris Tweed, first woven in the eighteenth century by crofters in the Outer Hebrides. In the 1840s, it was introduced to the British aristocracy and the cloth was used to make garments for the privileged to wear when hunting, shooting and fishing.

In 1909, the Harris Tweed Orb Certification Mark was created to protect against imitations. To qualify, the tweed must be woven on a hand-powered (not electric) loom by the islanders, and made from pure virgin wool dyed and spun in the Outer Hebrides.

> *A letter sent by a Scottish firm to a London merchant was misread*

POLO MINT

Polos were advertised in Britain as 'The Mint with the Hole'. They were first produced in 1948 by Rowntree, one of a small number of UK companies (including Cadbury of Creme Egg fame – see p.168) which were started in the nineteenth century by a Quaker family and run on philanthropic principles. But since 1998 the company has been owned by the Swiss giant Nestlé, who claim to make 38 million Polos every day. They also say it takes the weight of two elephants to press a Polo, though this does seem a rather primitive method of production.

Shaped like a lifebelt (and probably modelled on the Life Saver sweet in America), Polos have been made in other flavours, such as fruit and spearmint, but it is the white mint in a green-and-blue tube-shaped wrapper that has wormed its way so firmly into British affections. (For a while you could also buy small discs of the hard white mint, which were marketed as Polo holes.)

Consumers of Polos are typically split between 'crunchers', who bite into the hard mint, and 'suckers', who let the mint dissolve gradually in the mouth. Whether this difference has any psychological or social significance has, as far as we know, not yet been established.

People often suck a Polo mint to mask the smell of pungent foods like garlic or curry. Sometimes, though, sucking a Polo can be covering up something more serious, like the smell of alcohol as a person slinks home after a late-night drinking session, or perhaps to disguise the smell of perfume or after-shave after a secret meeting with an illicit lover.

Consumers of Polos are typically split between 'crunchers' and 'suckers'

BROMPTON BIKE

If you get on any train or bus, or step out onto any busy London street, there is a good chance you will see a Brompton bike. Why are Bromptons so popular? Because they are not just easy to fold up and carry, but also good to ride – and that makes them ideal for busy city commuters.

Perhaps the most unusual aspect of Bromptons is that they are still made in the UK, just 6 miles from Harrods (which is itself located on Brompton Road) in west London. The company is still British-owned and managed and the bikes themselves are sold all over the world.

The story of the Brompton has much in common with that of the Dyson vacuum cleaner (see p.94). The founder of the business, Andrew Ritchie, left university with a degree in Engineering and after a series of other jobs, happened to see the prototype of another manufacturer's folding bike and was immediately convinced he could do better.

With the financial support of some friends he produced the first prototypes in his bedroom looking out over the Brompton Oratory in South Kensington, London. Like Dyson, he initially thought of licensing his design to one of the more established bike manufacturers, but none of the major makers like Raleigh were interested. So, like Dyson, Andrew Ritchie set about making the bikes himself, also with the help of friends, who pre-ordered 30 bikes from him. Ritchie's big break came when the Brompton won the prestigious Best Product award at the 1987 Cyclex exhibition, against some strong international competition.

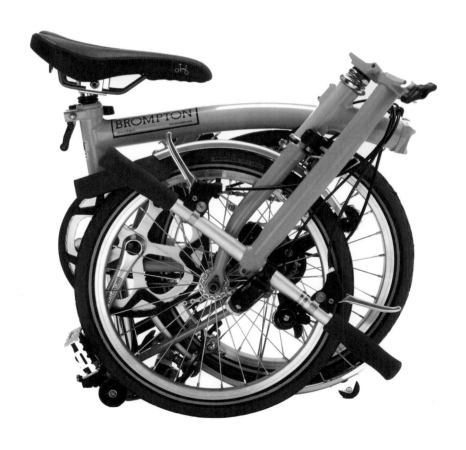

BAYONET LIGHT BULB

Everybody thinks they know who invented the first incandescent light bulb. It was Thomas Edison, right? The answer is: maybe. But if we were to ask: who was the first person to file a successful patent for the light bulb, the answer would be clearer. And it wasn't Thomas Edison. It was Joseph Swan (later Sir Joseph Swan), a British physicist and chemist, who filed the first patent in 1878. His house, in the north-east of England, was the first house anywhere in the world to be lit by electric light. And, in 1881, the Savoy Theatre in London was the first public building in the world to be illuminated entirely by electricity – using Swan's light bulbs, of course.

Edison was much more commercially minded than Swan – and that is perhaps why the American is better remembered than his British counterpart. The two inventors went on to set up the Edison & Swan United Electric Light Company, selling lamps made with a cellulose filament that Swan had invented in 1881. Edison went on to patent the Edison screw fitting, the type of screw-in bulb that is now used in most parts of the world.

Meanwhile, the bayonet fitting became the British standard and can also be found in other countries such as India, where Britain previously had influence. It is called a bayonet fitting for the simple reason that it is fitted using the same push-and-twist action used by a soldier to fit a bayonet on to a rifle.

As retailers like IKEA have introduced new light designs from abroad, many of which use screw-type fittings, so consumers in Britain have had to accept some change.

Fitted using the same push-and-twist action used by a soldier to fit a bayonet on to a rifle

BROWN SAUCE

Brown sauce is a popular accompaniment to the traditional English breakfast and one of the foods that British people living abroad say they miss most.

On the face of it, the idea of brown sauce is not very appetising, what with the colour's associations with sewers, mud and slurry, and it is true that the strong flavour of brown sauce is not to everyone's taste. It contains vinegar, tomatoes, sweeteners, dates, salt, tamarind, soy sauce, spices and onion extract – an amalgam of ingredients that combine the traditionally British with exotic new discoveries from far-flung parts of what was once the British Empire.

The original recipe for HP Sauce was created by Frederick Gibson Garton, a grocer from Nottingham. He registered the name HP Sauce in 1895, claiming that he had heard the sauce was being served in the restaurant in the Houses of Parliament. Other companies followed on, launching their own forms of brown sauce, and you will now find many brands on supermarket shelves, including Wilkin & Sons, shown here.

HP sauce gained more publicity in the 1960s when the wife of Prime Minister Harold Wilson revealed that her husband doused his food in it. It turned out later that this was not true, but by then the story had gained so much publicity that brown sauce in general became known as 'Wilson's gravy'. It seems Wilson was perfectly happy with this, as it enhanced his reputation as a man of the people.

The popularity of brown sauce continues to this day, even though we are all supposed to have become accomplished cooks with more sophisticated palates.

> **"**
> An amalgam of ingredients
> that combine the
> traditionally British with
> exotic new discoveries
> from far-flung parts

DARTBOARD

Darts became a popular game in England in the early part of the twentieth century and pub landlords and landladies were quick to pick up on it as a good way of attracting customers. But there were a few problems to resolve before it could become a major sport. First of all, each region in England had its own version of the game, which made it hard to run any kind of national competitions. And then there was the problem of the dartboard itself.

The dartboard is probably a descendant of the original archery target, scaled down for indoor play. Boards were originally made of wood, usually elm, cut from the end of a tree trunk. (The tree rings and radial cracks in the wood probably explain why the dartboard came to be laid out the way it is.) After each day's play the pub landlord or landlady would have to soak the wooden dartboard to heal the holes made by the darts, and to make it resistant to cracking. Even then chunks of wood would sometimes be pulled out of a board when a player extracted a dart.

The solution was presented by a company called Nodor. In 1932, they patented a new type of board – the bristle board, which did not crack and left no mark when the dart was pulled out. This new board was, however, quite expensive and did not completely replace the old wooden boards till the 1970s, when Dutch elm disease destroyed the supply of elm wood and growing affluence made the bristle boards more affordable.

Down at your local pub you will probably still find a dartboard and can engage in the same intensive work-out programme as top international darts players.

❝ *Chunks of wood would sometimes be pulled out of a board when a player extracted a dart* **❞**

ENGLISH MUSTARD

If you are accustomed to the kind of yellow mustard sauces served at American baseball venues, for example, then you could be in for a particularly nasty shock with English mustard. Just like chillies, English mustard can be deceptively strong. Take too much and you'll be left doubled up with your nose and eyes streaming.

Mustard is the original 'hot stuff'. No one knows for sure how phrases like 'to cut the mustard' (meaning: to be the best) and 'keen as mustard' (meaning: very enthusiastic) originated, but they both carry a strong and positive meaning. English mustard is among the strongest in the world, made from mustard flour, water, salt and, sometimes, lemon juice, but without the vinegar which makes other mustards rather milder.

There are many brands of English mustard on the market, but Colman's is probably the best known. Started in 1814 in Norwich, Colman's quickly grew and took over other producers, including Keen's. It was about 50 years later that the bull's head was added to the label, and this later became the company's trademark.

In 1926, Colman's ran one of the earliest 'teaser' marketing campaigns. The company put posters on London buses with the question 'Has Father Joined the Mustard Club?' but no other details. People rang the bus companies and the newspapers to find out about the club, which eventually released more details about itself. By the time the campaign was wound up in 1933 half a million membership badges had been issued.

Mustard is the original 'hot stuff'

HACKNEY CARRIAGE

Better known as a London taxi or black cab, the hackney carriage pictured opposite is as unmistakably British – and as essential a feature of any London street scene – as the red double-decker London bus (see p.82).

The London taxi, like all taxis, is called a hackney carriage because Hackney – a district long since absorbed into London – was once a village famous for breeding horses, including the working horses that were hired out to work the fields or pull carts and carriages. This is how the term hackney carriage came to be associated with a horse-drawn carriage available for hire, the forerunner of the present-day taxi. Modern taxis are no longer made in the area, though, instead being produced in Coventry.

Some people will tell you that there is still a law, the 1831 Hackney Carriage Act, which requires London taxi drivers to carry a bale of hay in their cabs. Sadly, the law simply requires taxi drivers to feed their horses themselves, but if they have no horse they do not have to carry the hay.

All taxi drivers in London have to acquire 'The Knowledge' before they can take to the streets, and you will sometimes see motorcyclists tootling round the streets on scooters or small motorbikes with a clipboard on their handlebars. These are trainee taxi drivers preparing to take their test. You might think that the advent of satnav would have made The Knowledge unnecessary. It certainly helps, but if you have ever taken a taxi during London rush hour, then you will have come to value The Knowledge as your driver dives up small alleyways barely wider than the cab itself and then emerges at the front of the jam.

> *All taxi drivers in London have to acquire 'The Knowledge'*

TENNIS RACQUET

For almost 100 years up to the 1970s, the frames of all tennis racquets were made of wood, and their strings were made from animal gut. Laminated wood construction had made racquets stronger but in the end they gave way to aluminium, carbon graphite, ceramics and titanium, whilst animal gut was replaced by modern synthetic materials.

The modern game of lawn tennis started life in Birmingham, around 1860, and its invention is now generally credited to Major Harry Gem and his friend Augurio Perera. Until that time tennis, or rackets as it was often called, was played indoors, bouncing the ball off walls as in present-day squash. It was Gem and Perera who took the game outdoors to the croquet lawn at Perera's house in Edgbaston and who then founded the world's first lawn tennis club in Leamington Spa in 1872.

In spite of this, neither Gem nor Perera is officially credited with inventing the game. That accolade goes to Major Walter Clopton Wingfield, who patented a game he called *sphairistikè* (from the Greek meaning 'skill at playing a ball'), or lawn tennis, in 1874. Luckily it was the name lawn tennis rather than *sphairistikè* that caught on.

It is Wingfield's name that appears in the International Tennis Hall of Fame and whose bust stands outside Wimbledon Lawn Tennis Club Museum. Whoever we credit as the inventor, the game soon gained popularity with the middle and upper classes and more clubs quickly sprang up. Wimbledon, or rather The All England Lawn Tennis and Croquet Club, was founded in 1868 (as the All England Croquet Club) and staged its first Lawn Tennis Championship in 1877, initially only for men, but followed just seven years later by a competition for women.

LONDON UNDERGROUND MAP

It is only when you see the earlier efforts at mapping the underground that you realise what is so clever about Harry Beck's 1931 design. Previous layouts tried to represent the underground more like a conventional geographical map, as though the ground had been X-rayed. The results were messy. Beck chose instead to use a schematic layout that is more geometric. He used clear colour coding for the different lines, but scale is only approximate.

There are no roads or landmarks. The only concession to what is on the surface is the inclusion of the River Thames.

The result is a clear and much-imitated design. The map has evolved as new underground lines have been added to the network, but it is still faithful to the original design. In 2009 Transport for London introduced a map that omitted the river but it had to be withdrawn after numerous complaints.

There are, of course, some drawbacks when you mess with scale, and if you are travelling around London you might want to arm yourself with a street map because some journeys will be quicker on foot, particularly if you take account of the amount of walking you have to do underground. For example, Leicester Square is only five minutes' walk from Covent Garden and Charing Cross to Embankment is about the same. Much as we love the old paper-based tube map, we have to acknowledge that it works just as well on a smartphone, as shown here. And the addition of apps that work out your best route and tell you about hold-ups swings the balance in favour of newer technology. But that takes nothing away from the genius of the original design.

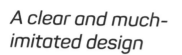

A clear and much-imitated design

CUSTARD

Custard is made from milk or cream, and egg yolk. It can be a thin pouring sauce (sometimes called crème anglaise) or a thick jelly-like mixture of the kind used in custard tarts or slices. Custards baked in pastry were enjoyed as long ago as the Middle Ages, but it was in the 1840s that custard itself really became popular.

That was after Alfred Bird invented custard powder for his wife, who was allergic to eggs. Bird used cornflour instead to thicken the sauce and soon discovered that he had a potential bestseller on his hands. Bird set about marketing it vigorously and Bird's Custard Powder became very successful, its light weight before hydration making it ideal for transportation on ships heading out to the British colonies.

Today, British consumers are more likely to buy ready-made custard, which they simply have to heat up and serve. In pubs custard makes a popular dessert, served as an accompaniment to apple crumble or, even better, sticky toffee pudding, a sponge made with thick toffee sauce. The kind of dessert you eat because, as your grandmother would have said, 'Your eyes are just too big for your stomach.'

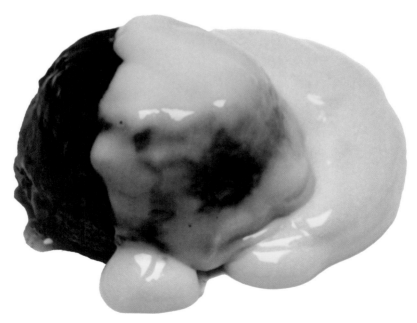

JCB 3CX

JCB belongs to that small list of companies – like Hoover – that come to define not just their own product but the whole category in which they operate. The company created the first mechanical digger – sometimes called a backhoe loader – in 1953 and since then JCB has become a generic term covering any tractor that has a bucket at the front and a digger at the back.

Up and down the length of Britain, and all over the world, you will see JCB's distinctive yellow machines excavating foundations on building sites, carving trenches along roads, digging ditches on farms, shifting rocks in quarries, or even clearing rubble after an earthquake. Its current 3CX model shown here is a direct descendant of the iconic 3C model of the 1960s, the backhoe loader that really made JCB's name.

The company was started in 1945 by Joseph Cyril Bamford, who gave it his initials (JCB) along with his genius for practical invention. That was the year when he welded together scrap steel to make and sell his first piece of equipment – a farm trailer. But Bamford was not only a gifted engineer. He was also a talented marketer.

He developed the company's crisp black on yellow logo early in its history and maintained the company's reputation carefully, aware that it was not enough for JCBs just to be highly functional pieces of equipment. Bamford understood his customers and sought to make their lives easier; for example, every 3C came with an electric kettle that could be plugged into the cab. A thoughtful touch.

*Not just highly functional
pieces of equipment*

HOT AND COLD TAPS

Many visitors to Britain are struck by the common use of separate hot and cold taps. In fact, our plumbing seems to be a major source of fascination to them, particularly if they stay in an older 'bed and breakfast' or hotel.

Even though the first mixer tap was patented as long ago as 1880, most older houses in Britain are still equipped with separate taps, and we even continue to fit them in new houses to this day.

Mostly, however, the mixer tap has arrived and is now common in new kitchens and bathrooms, but many still prefer their taps to be separate. You know where you are with separate taps. No risk of filling your drinking glass with a stream of warm water if you have a separate cold tap. But be careful. As there is no specified standard layout for fitting the two taps, you cannot be sure which tap is which, unless they are clearly marked.

And if you come from southern Europe you may expect 'C' on a tap to tell you that it will produce hot water (C for *chaud*, *caliente* or *caldo*), whereas of course it will be the 'C' for cold tap. Choose the wrong tap and it will be better than a strong coffee to wake you on a winter's morning.

*" Plumbing seems to be a
major source of fascination "*

MAGNOLIA PAINT

A kind of pale pinkish shade – not quite white, not quite peach – magnolia is to British house decorators as grass is to cows: it is everywhere and they never tire of it.

Every now and then a weekend newspaper colour supplement will run an article in which a designer will present bold new colours. An estate agent may extol the virtues of making your house stand out by selective use of bold colours, and there will be spreads of celebrities proudly showing how they (meaning their interior decorator) have made tasteful use of colour in their expensively decorated luxury home.

The truth, though, is that Britain is one of the most densely populated countries in the world and that most British homes are therefore relatively small. And there is a continuing trend towards small, single-occupancy flats, so they will probably become smaller still. In a small room bright, deep colours can become oppressive, whereas pale, neutral colours add a sense of space and provide a blank canvas for displaying paintings and large-scale photographs. And the British, for all their creativity in music and the arts, can be very conservative indeed in their domestic tastes. Magnolia paint is here to stay.

Back in the late 1950s, road signs were inconsistent and often hard to read; many dated back to the 1920s and looked old-fashioned. Two graphic designers, Jock Kinneir and Margaret Calvert, were commissioned to come up with a standardised and modern system of signage, one that could cope with the emerging motorway age.

Their solution was to create two new typefaces: Transport, which is used on most of the current road signs to this day, and Motorway, a variant of Transport which is still used on all the distinctive blue signs on British motorways. Where

towns and cities on the previous road signs used all capital letters, Kinneir and Calvert chose a mix of capitals and lower case. They also simplified the language used. 'HALT – MAJOR ROAD AHEAD' became simply 'STOP'. The changes were the result of rigorous testing. Signs were propped up against trees around London's Hyde Park and they assessed how easy they were to read.

At the same time they devised a set of graphic symbols that would convey the necessary message quickly and effectively to a driver moving at speed. The only sign that Calvert wished she had done differently is the one that people like best: the 'men at work' sign, which shows a man pushing a shovel into a pile of sand (shown here), and which inspired an album by the musician Viv Stanshall called *Men Opening Umbrellas Ahead*. Not many road signs have had music written in their honour.

BELISHA BEACON

The Belisha beacon is an orange flashing globe on top of a black-and-white-striped post, always found either side of zebra crossings (which are pedestrian road crossings marked by black and white stripes on the road surface). Probably the most famous zebra crossing in Britain appears on the cover of The Beatles' 1969 *Abbey Road* album, but the Belisha beacons cannot be seen because they are out of sight at the sides of the road.

In the early days of motoring, pedestrian crossings were simply marked by metal studs across the road. Then, in 1934, the Transport Minister – the wonderfully named Leslie Hore-Belisha – decided that they were not easy enough to see. So he added the distinctive lights and donated half his surname to them.

It was only in the early 1950s that the white stripes were painted on the road to create the zebra crossing. For the overseas visitor the critical point is that car drivers are legally required to stop at a zebra crossing, and British motorists are generally good at observing this law.

Many British people are barely aware of the existence of zebra crossings with Belisha beacons. This is partly because they are such a common feature of any urban landscape, but also because many zebra crossings have now been replaced by pelican crossings, the difference being that pelicans use conventional traffic lights to control the traffic, which are activated by the pedestrian pressing a button at the roadside.

Toucan, puffin and tiger crossings also exist (once road planners had started the wildlife theme it seems they couldn't let go of it): toucan crossings allow pedestrians and cyclists to cross the road at the same time; puffin crossings are the same as pelican ones, but with sensors attached; and tiger crossings are for cyclists only.

> **"**
> *He added the
> distinctive lights
> and donated half his
> surname to them*

GLAMPING TENT

'Glamping' is short for 'glamorous camping'. Visitors to the infamous Glastonbury music festival no longer have to accept the standard mud and discomfort. Anyone who has several thousand pounds or so available to spend on the weekend can stay in style, perhaps renting a shikar tent (like those used by the Maharajah of Jodhpur for hunting trips). Such tents accommodate a king-sized bed with Egyptian cotton sheets, duck-down duvets and 'jewel-spangled Rajasthani covers'. The floors are covered in sheepskin. And no more queuing for the malodorous loos; for a bit more money you can order your own en-suite toilet plumbed into the tent for your exclusive use.

But glamping is not confined to music festivals. All over the country campsites quite unlike those known to our parents are springing up. At Cuckoo Down Farm in Devon, for example, you can rent an 18-foot diameter yurt with a wooden floor, furnished with rugs, a double bed, two double sofa beds plus cushions, a coffee table, storage chests and a wood-burning stove. And not to forget: an eco-friendly compost toilet as well. Or if you still feel that is too demanding, there is now a wide range of traditional gypsy caravans to hire around the country.

For your wedding you can now choose to hold the happy event in a marquee and then employ Tobyn Cleeves' Hotel Bell Tent service to provide luxury bell tents, like the one pictured here, for your guests to sleep in, free of the worries of getting back to a hotel after a day of celebration.

RANGE ROVER

Today's Range Rover is very different from the car that was launched in 1970. The original car had vinyl seats and rubber mats on the floor. It was designed to be a working vehicle on a farm or estate in the morning, climbing effortlessly over fields, hills and rough ground, and a comfortable road vehicle in the afternoon; at home in both town and country, and above all: practical. Shortly after it was launched in 1970, it appeared in an exhibition at the Louvre, where it was described as an 'exemplary work of industrial design'.

It was later that the car acquired its cachet of luxury, with burr walnut veneers, leather seats and deep-pile carpets. Many credit the Range Rover with being the first luxury SUV (Sports Utility Vehicle), though the Jeep Wagoneer arguably pioneered that category some years before the first Range Rover appeared.

Bearing out the Range Rover's ruggedness and off-road ability it immediately became the vehicle of choice for long-distance overland expeditions, including the 1972 British Trans-Americas Expedition. In this event two Range Rovers travelled the length of North and South America, from Alaska to Argentina, including the traversing of the notorious Darién Gap that straddles Panama and Colombia, where there are no roads for 250 miles. It also became a popular vehicle, together with other Land Rover off-roaders, in the Camel Trophy, which ran over various challenging terrains around the world between 1980 and 2000.

Today the Range Rover remains a highly competent off-road vehicle, with an exceptional capability to negotiate difficult terrain, even though most drivers never tackle more than the occasional snow-covered road or potholed track.

*An exemplary work
of industrial design*

CRICKET BAT AND BALL

The laws of cricket date back to 1788 and were drawn up by the Marylebone Cricket Club (MCC), which is based at Lord's Cricket Ground in London. There are 42 laws in total, each covering a different aspect of the game. So, for example, Law 5 specifies the weight and size of the ball, while Law 6 prescribes the dimensions of the bat. It also states that the bat must be made only of wood, and usually that wood will be white willow, which is treated with linseed oil to protect it.

The cricket bat has evolved over the centuries and until 1979 no one thought it necessary to spell out that it should be made of wood, but in that year an Australian player, Dennis Lillee, tried to use an aluminium bat, which was promptly outlawed. Similar changes to the laws have been made to restrict the use of other technical enhancements such as carbon fibre in the handle.

This contrasts strongly with tennis, where wood has long since been superseded by more advanced materials.

The ball is also unique, with its leather surface and raised welt of stitching. Being able to judge the state of the ball and how it will behave on a given pitch as the game progresses is a key part of the skill of the game.

Law 42 in cricket captures the British attitude to rules in sport perfectly. It puts the responsibility for ensuring fairness squarely on the shoulders of the team captains, but also states that the umpires are the sole judges of fair and unfair play. Not just that, but if either umpire (there are always two) considers an action to be unfair, even if it is not specifically covered by the laws of cricket, then he can intervene.

"

Law 42 in cricket captures the British attitude to rules in sport perfectly

ROLLS-ROYCE PHANTOM

Rolls-Royce is a name that whispers luxury, prestige and quality. Where a Ferrari is like an Italian tenor personifying style and speed, Rolls-Royce is the dignified aristocrat who quietly assumes privilege as a right. It is possible to love a Rolls-Royce and hate it at the same time: admire its engineering excellence, delight in its understated elegance; yet despise the exclusivity and the unwarranted assumptions of superiority that it conveys on its owner.

For ten years in the 1920s Rolls-Royce built cars in Springfield, Massachusetts, but customers wanted them to be made in Britain, so they closed the factory. The cars are now made at a factory which opened in 2003 in Sussex, near to the historic Goodwood motor and horse racing tracks and to Goodwood House, the stately home of the Dukes of Richmond for several centuries. This is Rolls-Royce's homeland.

Charles Rolls and Henry Royce met in 1904. Rolls was an enthusiast of cars and aeroplanes – relishing the speed and excitement that they offered to the wealthy in those pioneering days. He provided the finance and business acumen needed, but died in 1910 in a flying accident when the tail broke off his plane. Royce was the engineering brains, dedicated to excellence. His commitment is summed up in his motto: 'Whatever is rightly done, however humble, is noble.' It was Royce himself who carried on and built the business, including taking it into the making of aero engines, outliving his business partner by over 20 years.

> **Whatever is rightly done,
> however humble, is noble**

DAVID MELLOR CUTLERY

Stainless steel was perfected by Harry Brearley in Sheffield around 1913. Through to the 1980s Sheffield continued to be a centre for the development of modern high-strength low-alloy steels. At their peak, more than half the population of Sheffield was involved in the steel and cutlery industries, but from the 1980s on it has struggled to compete with emerging low-cost centres of production around the world.

There are, however, some businesses that have survived: companies that have adapted and focused on the higher added-value ends of their markets. One is Sheffield Forgemasters, founded in 1805, which enjoys a global reputation for producing large complex steel forgings and castings.

Another is David Mellor Design. The founder of the company, David Mellor was born in Sheffield in 1930 and made his name in cutlery, but he was also a talented designer

of other products, with credits for furniture, tools, ecclesiastical silver and even traffic lights, a bus shelter and a square postbox.

Mellor's earliest range of cutlery, Pride, was designed when he was a student at the Royal College of Art in the 1950s and remains in production to this day. Another range, English, was originally made as a commission for 10 Downing Street, who required cutlery for ceremonial dining.

Not all of Mellor's designs were successful. His square postbox, designed in 1966, had many practical features, for example a system that allowed quick emptying of the box by the postman. The public rebelled, however, more comfortable with the circular pillar box, and Mellor's square boxes were withdrawn after only 200 had been installed. His traffic lights proved much more successful, and his design is still in use today.

> *At their peak, more than half the population of Sheffield was involved in the steel and cutlery industries*

GUY FAWKES MASK

The fifth of November is known as Guy Fawkes Night, or Bonfire Night, and in cities, towns and villages across Britain communities get together to light a bonfire and set off fireworks. On the top of each bonfire will be a guy – a stuffed dummy – often dressed to resemble Guy Fawkes, a man who died over 400 years ago.

Guy Fawkes was a member of a group of English Catholics who plotted to blow up the Houses of Parliament and kill King James I in 1605. Unfortunately for Fawkes, he was captured while guarding the stockpile of gunpowder in the space under the Palace of Westminster, and he was sentenced to be hanged. On 5 November, 1605, Londoners were encouraged to celebrate the King's escape from assassination by lighting bonfires, and every 5 November from that day on was marked as a day of thanksgiving for 'the joyful day of deliverance'.

Part of the tradition includes children making their own guy by stuffing straw or newspaper into old clothes and making a mask for it, then requesting passers-by to give a 'penny for the guy'. As inflation eroded the value of a penny this increased to a pound before the tradition started to die away.

The anti-hero in Alan Moore's graphic novel *V for Vendetta* uses a Guy Fawkes mask as he battles against a fascist state, and it is that image that has been used by anti-Wall Street protesters, presumably because they seek, like Guy Fawkes, to shake the foundations of the Establishment. Ironically the *V for Vendetta* image is now owned by Time Warner, a major global media company, and each mask bought by an anti-establishment protester pays a royalty to them.

> *Part of the tradition includes children making their own guy by stuffing straw or newspaper into old clothes and making a mask for it*

BROGUE SHOE

The brogue is a style of shoe whose main distinguishing characteristic is small holes punched into the leather uppers. It is a sturdy piece of footwear, originally from Scotland or Ireland, and the word comes from the Gaelic for shoe.

To begin with, brogues were simply regarded as practical, strong, outdoor, country walking-shoes mainly intended for men, but over time they have become acceptable as smart shoes for use at social or business occasions, and ranges have been extended to include styles for women. If you want to master the brogue you will have to get to grips with several styles: full brogues, semi-brogues, quarter brogues and longwing brogues, with four styles of closure: Oxford, Derby, ghillie and monk strap. Or you could just pick some you like.

Britain has a strong tradition of shoe manufacturing, mainly centred in the East Midlands around Northampton. Many of the long-established companies have now closed or been sold to foreign buyers, but a few survive. Loake, founded in 1880, continues to operate as a family-owned business, making brogues and other shoe styles at its Kettering factory; not far away, Joseph Cheaney & Sons, another family-owned business set up in the 1880s, continues to make brogues and other shoes in its factory in the small market town of Desborough; Grenson started in 1866 and still operates out of the factory it built in Rushden in 1895; and Sanders & Sanders, founded in 1873, also continues to thrive in that same town.

What each has in common is a focus on high-quality shoes that transcend fashion or fad, the kind of shoes favoured by wearers who buy them even during recessions.

BAGPIPES

If you are not a fan then there are just two types of bagpipe: the deafening and the not-quite-so-loud. Or to put it another way: mouth-blown pipes like the Great Highland bagpipes shown here, which are best played outdoors (unless, as one expert on Celtic musical instruments put it, you happen to live in an aircraft hangar); and their smaller cousins, parlour pipes, which can be mouth-blown or bellows-blown, and which can be played indoors.

Bagpipes, in a wide variety of different designs, can be found all over the world, including – no doubt to the horror of many Scots – in England, where there are even carvings of pipers playing their instruments to be found in many old cathedrals. But, whereas in England the bagpiping traditions are no longer maintained very strongly, in Scotland they continue to thrive.

There are more than 250 types of bagpipes played around the world today, from Sweden to China. Indeed the first documented bagpipe was found not in Scotland, but in Turkey, and dates back to 1000 BC. In spite of this, it is Scotland's Great Highland bagpipes that are the most renowned. So much so, that it is hard to think about bagpipes without also picturing a Scottish pipe band wearing kilts, sporrans, tassels and thick hose. And it is only in Scotland that they are used in a military manner; bagpipes in other countries are usually used solely to accompany dancing (as they also are in Scotland, of course).

There are more than 250 types of bagpipes played around the world today

ARGOS CATALOGUE

To most people outside Britain, Argos is an ancient city in Greece whose history stretches back to 5000 BC, which rivalled Sparta in its heyday and which is famous for its ancient temple: the Heraion of Argos.

To anyone living in Britain since 1973, Argos is a shop found on most British high streets, famous for its weighty literary tome: the richly illustrated catalogue of Argos.

When Argos opened its first shop over 40 years ago the concept was revolutionary for British consumers. Instead of displaying goods in its windows and around the shop, Argos kept all the products in boxes in a warehouse at the back of the store and customers chose from a catalogue, taking their order on a slip of paper to the counter, then waiting for the item to be collected from the warehouse.

Over the years the Argos catalogue has charted the shift in consumer tastes and technologies, from typewriters, Polaroid cameras and Spectrum computers – all now long gone – through Sony Walkman, video players and compact sunbeds to popular gadgets – Apple iPads, and so on.

The Argos catalogue once graced the shelves of most British homes, but today its customers are just as likely to go online to search for what they want. The Argos website is one of the most heavily used in the country, with millions of hits every month, popular because buyers can check to see if the product is in stock at their local store and reserve it for collection.

"

The Argos catalogue has charted the shift in consumer tastes and technologies

MR WHIPPY ICE CREAM VAN

Until the 1960s, almost the only way to eat ice cream at home was to buy it from an ice cream van. These vans would tour the suburban streets of Britain playing a tinny version of 'Greensleeves' through some cheap speakers. And even when homeowners started to acquire freezers, ice cream vans continued to roam the residential streets on summer evenings and at weekends. Their plinky-plonk music carries a nostalgic magic for anyone who was a child at that time.

The ice cream van survives to this day, but is now more likely to be found at a sporting event, at a show or at the seaside than it is touring suburban streets in search of business. In spite of this, though, they are still a regular sight and children still respond to their chimes with the same excitement that their parents did.

The Mr Whippy van is special because it not only sells pre-packaged ice cream and lollies, but also the kind of soft ice cream that is pumped from a machine directly into a cone, topped off with a Cadbury flake to create an ice cream known universally as a 99. This kind of soft ice cream was developed by a research team that reputedly included Margaret Thatcher – in the days when she was a chemist rather than Prime Minister.

The Mr Whippy van shown here is a restored 1950s van still selling 99s today in the Leeds area of northern England.

> **"** *Their plinky-plonk music carries a nostalgic magic for anyone who was a child at that time* **"**

DOG POO BIN

Since 1891, Britain has been the home of what claims to be the world's largest dog show – Crufts. It is now held every March in Birmingham. Hosting 28,000 dogs, it allows owners and breeders to compete for the coveted 'Best in Breed' award.

Not surprisingly, the obsessive British love of dogs, and the large number of overfed pets that British people now own, present some unique problems. One of the biggest is that they produce an estimated 1,000 tonnes of dog poo every day. The problem of dog dirt on the streets became so bad that in 2005 the government passed a new law, The Clean Neighbourhoods and Environment Act. This law obliges dog owners to clean up after their pets, giving rise to the dog poo bag – a small, usually black, plastic bag – and the dog poo bin, a relatively recent addition to many of Britain's streets, into which owners should deposit the used bags. Owners who fail to clear up are liable to a steep fine.

One in four of all cats and dogs is now reckoned to be overweight – not unlike many of their owners. Not just that, but more and more owners in Britain are treating their dogs like people, so apart from overfeeding them, they are pampering them with all kinds of luxuries, like 'super premium foods' such as venison or rabbit – gourmet meat dishes sold not in tins but in attractive plastic bowls – all of which presumably helps produce a higher grade of poo.

> *Owners who fail to clear up are liable to a steep fine*

RED PILLAR BOX

The red pillar box is the traditional free-standing postbox used in the UK. It is one of the most enduring everyday designs on our streets. The first ones were installed in the Channel Islands in 1852 and were soon adopted across mainland Britain. Before that time anyone wanting to post a letter would have had to take it to a special receiving house or post office. Later postbox designs included a Time of Collection (TOC) plaque, which continues to this day.

There have been a number of different designs over the years – some square, some with six or eight sides, some oval, one design like a fluted Greek column; but the most common, the National Standard Design, is cylindrical with a domed top. Attempts to modernise the design in the 1960s were not well received by the public and most were withdrawn, leaving the older designs in place.

Like all everyday icons, the red pillar box has suffered its fair share of abuse. In 1939, the Irish Republican Army (IRA) embarked on a short-lived campaign to sabotage the British economy by posting letter bombs inside letter boxes in London, Birmingham and Manchester. There is no record of any deaths resulting from these bombs. The cast-iron construction of the pillar box, along with its deep foundations, makes it extremely strong. So much so that when the IRA detonated a large bomb in the centre of Manchester in 1996 there was considerable damage to surrounding buildings but the Victorian pillar box, installed in 1887, survived without damage.

> **"**
> *The cast-iron construction of the pillar box, along with its deep foundations, makes it extremely strong*

POST

MORRIS DANCERS' BELLS AND HAT

The word 'morris' comes from the French *morisque* or Flemish *morisch*; the earliest historical record of morris dancing dates back to 1448 and it was already considered an ancient form of dance by Elizabethan times. In the winter of 1600 the Shakespearean actor William Kemp morris-danced from London to Norwich, a distance of well over 100 miles, drawing out large welcoming crowds along the way. He later chronicled this in his *Nine Daies Wonder*, subtitled: 'Performed in a dance from London to Norwich. Containing the pleasure, pains and kind entertainment of William Kemp between London and that City in his late Morrice.'

The costumes and objects used in dancing vary from region to region. The hat and bells shown here are those worn by the Adlington Morris Men in Cheshire, the bells being worn round the calves, along with criss-cross ribbons worn across the chest, known as baldrics. Morris dances may feature waved handkerchiefs or sticks, or in some cases swords.

The fortunes of morris dancing have risen and fallen, prospering in villages and then declining during the Industrial Revolution as people moved into the cities in search of work. It recovered again when Queen Victoria celebrated her Golden Jubilee in 1887 but then declined once more after World War One following the deaths of so many of its young performers, only to recover once more in the 1960s and 1970s when interest in folk music and customs was renewed. For all the jokes people make about morris dancers, people do still love to see them, and groups are always in great demand at local festivities, especially through the summer months.

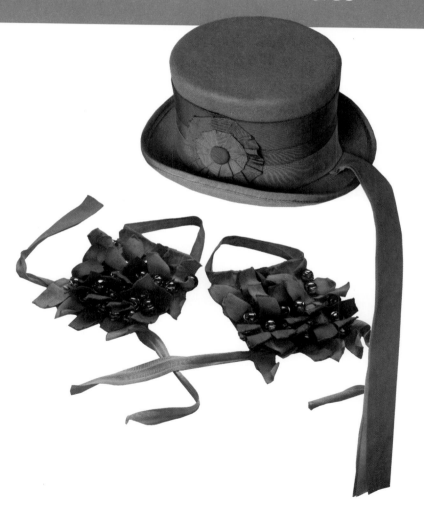

CADBURY CREME EGG

The Creme Egg is a chocolate egg whose thick shell contains a gooey white and yellow fondant filling, resembling the white and yolk of a real egg. The makers, Cadbury, claim that Creme Eggs are the best-selling confectionery item in the UK between New Year's Day and Easter.

Started in 1824 by John Cadbury, the business grew quickly. Cadbury was not just an able businessman but also a Quaker and, like many members of non-conformist Christian groups at that time, was prevented from attending university and so turned his energy and intellect towards business instead. Having very strict moral principles he rejected alcohol and insisted on selling products of high purity and to the correct measure (at a time when this was not always the case). He also believed it was the duty of all men to help their neighbours, and he provided pensions and medical care for his employees and their families long before this became common practice.

In Bournville, in Birmingham, he built a village of attractive, well-built homes for his workers, each with a garden to enable them to grow vegetables. Now controlled by the Bournville Trust and entirely separate from the Cadbury company (which is now American-owned), Bournville remains a model of town planning to this day.

John Cadbury's Victorian model of philanthropic business dealings was not unique. Another Quaker chocolate maker, Rowntree, (now also foreign-owned – by Nestlé) followed similar philanthropic principles, but Cadbury led the way, and that above all is why it remains such a respected name in Britain.

The best-selling confectionery item in the UK between New Year's Day and Easter

PANTOMIME DAME'S COSTUME

Pantomime is a very British form of entertainment. Traditionally performed at Christmas time, pantomime is a popular form of theatre for family audiences. Based loosely on a traditional fairy tale like Cinderella or Snow White, it will always include the following ingredients: music, songs, dancing, clowning around, cross-dressing, slapstick, topical jokes, audience participation, some traditional catchphrases, and a bit of mild sexual innuendo.

Children soon learn to participate in the rituals of pantomime, which include booing at the villain (there is always a baddy); and at some point the characters on stage will engage in an argument that involves one character shouting 'Oh, yes it is!' and another shouting 'Oh no, it isn't!' with support from the audience. The slapstick will usually include one character hiding behind the other

with the audience shouting out 'He's behind you!'

The pantomime dame is the key player in the whole experience. A good dame is the anchor for a successful pantomime, and she will always be played by a man. To add comic effect she wears huge brightly coloured dresses stuffed with masses of padding to create a 'fuller figure', along with visible frilly underwear, and topped off with lashings of make-up on her face… and an extravagant coloured wig. In short: a man who is so obviously trying to play a woman that no one could possibly think it really was a woman. Quite why the pantomime dame is played by a man (and the male hero by a woman) no one really knows, though it may date from Shakespearean times when women did not appear on stage. Whatever the explanation, this playful form of cross-dressing is all part of the fun.

"
Oh no, it isn't!

BARRISTER'S WIG

For hundreds of years British judges and lawyers have worn a hat or wig on their heads when in court. In early Tudor times it was a black flat bonnet or cap, but they started wearing wigs around 1680, 20 years after Charles II returned to England from exile in France, bringing the fashion with him. The word wig itself is short for periwig, derived from the French word for a wig, *perruque*.

Wigs had been popular in the French court and so became associated with the ruling classes. Courtiers would compete with one another to wear the most extravagant wigs and even today we use the term 'bigwig' to describe someone who is particularly important, or at least thinks they are. The use of wigs at that (less hygienic) time was probably also associated with covering up hair loss, dandruff or unattractive scalp conditions.

For 150 years the legal wig was usually of powdered white or grey hair, which needed a lot of care – curling, perfuming and powdering – to keep it in usable condition. In 1822, Humphrey Ravenscroft invented a legal wig made of pale horsehair that was much easier to maintain and look after, and the firm of Ede & Ravenscroft still makes the wigs worn by barristers and judges in court today.

Wigs ceased to be fashionable in society at large by 1800, but they have continued to be used in the British legal profession (and in countries whose legal systems are based on the British system of law).

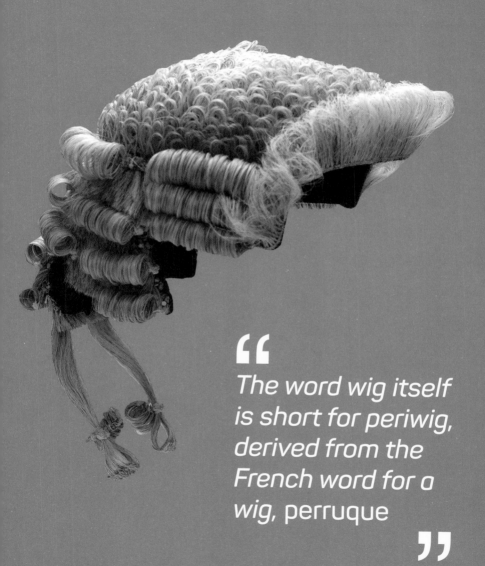

> **"** The word wig itself is short for periwig, derived from the French word for a wig, perruque **"**

'QUEUE THIS WAY' SIGN

The British tend to be pretty stoic, a quality that has seen them through some difficult times, like the dark days of World War Two when defeat looked likely and food was short. They also have a strong sense of justice, sometimes referred to as a belief in 'fair play', no doubt related to their fondness for creating sports like cricket, football and rugby and drawing up the rules by which they are run. Bring those two things – stoicism and a sense of fairness – together and you get an explanation for the British fondness for queuing.

For most British people, it is simply that they like to have things well ordered and as stress-free as possible. The simple principle that if you arrive first then it is fair that you get served first ensures this – provided, of course, that everyone else plays by the same rules.

The Times writer Matt Rudd decided to report on the royal wedding in 2011 by joining the crowds lined up along the Mall in front of Buckingham Palace. After waiting in an orderly line-up for 21 hours there was suddenly a stampede of people from behind him, including two Americans who, riding roughshod over Rudd's British sensibilities, elbowed their way past him, noting to one another that 'the trouble with these Brits is that they don't know how to push to the front'. Disgusted, he set off home, missing the royal couple's balcony kiss.

FULTON UMBRELLA

Arnold Fulton was an engineer and inventor who started making umbrellas in 1956 in London, and the company he founded has now grown to be the largest supplier of umbrellas in the UK. Its current range includes a wide variety of different umbrellas – golf, folding, men's, women's and traditional walking umbrellas, as well as the more colourful designer-style range, one of which is shown here – taken from Fulton's Morris & Co. collection.

The umbrella, sometimes also referred to as a 'brolly', is not a British invention – although a British inventor, Samuel Fox, did patent the first wire-frame collapsible umbrella in 1842. References to umbrellas have been found in China dating back to earlier than 200 BC (including an actual carriage umbrella amongst the Terracotta Warriors at X'ian), as well as in documents found in the Middle East and Greece. Mostly these were parasols (the word umbrella derives from the Latin for shade), but in Britain it has to be said they are more likely to be used to protect from that regular feature of the British climate – rain.

The umbrella only started to be used in Britain in the 1750s, initially viewed with some suspicion and dismissed as a French fashion. However, its practical benefits soon outweighed any doubts. The traditional image of the London city gent is of a tall man in a bowler hat and pinstripe Savile Row suit with a furled long black umbrella hooked over his arm. But much has changed over the last 50 years. The bowler hat has gone, the typical City worker is likely to be more casually dressed than their New York counterpart, and the umbrella may well be a compact version.

Initially viewed with some suspicion and dismissed as a French fashion

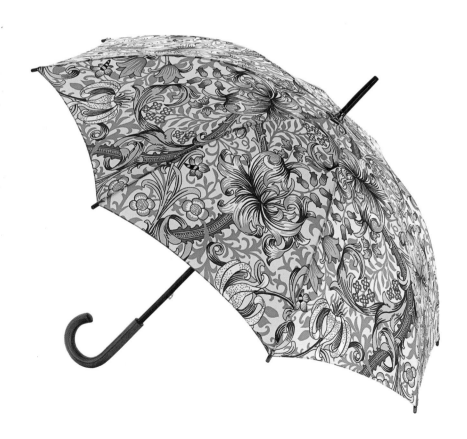

FULL ENGLISH BREAKFAST

The full English will include some or all of the following: fried egg, bacon, sausage, fried bread, fried mushrooms and grilled tomato, with the possible option of black pudding (especially in northern England), haggis (Scotland – see p.76), laverbread (Wales – see p.93), as well as hash browns and baked beans. This may be preceded by porridge (especially in Scotland) or cereals, and should be followed by toast and chunky orange marmalade if you are to do the job properly. And wash it all down with a mug of strong English breakfast tea (or coffee if you insist).

This can of course end up being a very substantial meal, which will probably keep you going till lunchtime at least. Approach it by following the old proverb: 'Breakfast like a King, lunch like a Prince, dine like a poor man', and you will be fine.

To be clear, this is not the typical British person's daily breakfast. Half the working population admit that they do not eat breakfast at all, grabbing a snack later on instead.

The full English is more a treat saved up for times when we are staying at a hotel or 'bed and breakfast'. Nothing can compare with a nice lie-in followed by a full breakfast – cooked by someone else of course. Cooking it yourself at home on a weekday? Not likely.

ROYAL MAIL RUBBER BAND

It was a Briton, Stephen Perry, who invented the first rubber band. He patented it on 17 March 1845. His invention is one of the 'hidden heroes' of everyday life: a deceptively simple object that, like the paper clip and adhesive tape, makes our lives easier though most of us take it for granted.

In 2004, the Royal Mail introduced biodegradable rubber bands, using them to bundle letters together for delivery, and it was soon getting through some 800 million of them a year. Not surprising, then, that a fair number ended up on the streets. In 2005, stung by criticism about the number of rubber bands littering British towns and cities, it had the bright idea of using *red* bands instead of the usual brown, hoping that postmen would see them more easily and so pick them up if dropped.

Sadly, that was not what happened. The postmen continued to drop them in large numbers, but, because they were red, everyone else noticed them too.

Some wondered if the discarded rubber band was the Royal Mail's equivalent of a dog weeing on a tree: to mark out their territory. It was suggested that perhaps they wanted to scare off the new privately operated couriers by showing them that the Royal Mail had already got the area covered. Others speculated that the postmen feared getting lost, and so – just in case they suffered sudden and severe memory loss – dropped the rubber bands so that they could follow their trail back to the post office.

M&S UNDERWEAR

Michael Marks and Tom Spencer started their company in the 1890s. Marks was an immigrant from present-day Belarus who set out as a market trader in Leeds, while Spencer was a bookkeeper from Yorkshire.

What made them such an established part of British culture was the their reputation for selling clothes of dependable quality at reasonable prices, as well as their policy of selling only UK-made clothing and accepting returned goods without any challenge.

But some customers have been less than satisfied. In 2008, the TV presenter Jeremy Paxman complained that M&S socks wore out faster and did not stay up as well as they once had. But it was the underwear that drew his sharpest criticism. In an email to the M&S chief executive he wrote that M&S pants 'no longer provide adequate support. When I've discussed this with friends… it has revealed widespread gusset anxiety. I do feel that someone should take up this mighty battle.'

Whilst this criticism from a well-known television presenter no doubt hurt, you can see it as a measure of the affection that M&S still holds in many people's hearts. Why else would Paxman bother to write to the company when he could have just bought his underwear from somewhere else?

When I've discussed this with friends... it has revealed widespread gusset anxiety

STILE

A stile is a simple structure, usually made of wood, that you will find on footpaths all over Britain. It provides access through or over fences and hedges for walkers, but keeps animals in their place and, unlike a gate, cannot be left open.

Stiles take many forms, but usually consist of one or two steps over a fence, as shown here, or occasionally adopt a V shape that the walker has to squeeze through.

In the past, stiles were installed on footpaths provided for farmworkers and others to walk from village to village, but today they are mostly used for leisure walking, the result of more than 100 years of campaigning to allow public access to the countryside. It all began as long ago as 1884 when James Bryce MP introduced a bill calling for freedom to roam the countryside. By that time the railways had made it possible for people working in the cities to get out into the country at weekends, but the bill met strong resistance from private landowners and it failed to make it into law.

In 1932, a mass protest by ramblers at Kinder Scout in the Peak District of England led to six people being jailed. Finally, in 1949, the National Parks were created and subsequent legislation – most recently the Countryside and Rights of Way (CROW) Act in 2000 – opened up access for people to roam the British countryside.

It all began as long ago as 1884 when James Bryce MP introduced a bill calling for freedom to roam the countryside

CAR NUMBER PLATE

British car number plates have to be white at the front of the car and yellow at the back, and use black letters (using a font known as Charles Wright 2001, if you are a student of typefaces). Why they are white at one end and yellow at the other we do not know. Maybe it helps you tell which way the car is pointing?

And if you are a little bit nerdy then you will want to know that the numbering system uses two letters, followed by two numbers and then three letters. The first letter tells you where the car was first registered, so for example you C tells you it is from Cymru (Wales), S from Scotland, L from London, M from Manchester and so on. The two numbers in the middle tell you when the car was first registered.

If you do not mind paying a bit more money, you can make your car stand out by ordering a personalised plate. To boost national income the government sells off some 'interesting' number plates by auction. Specially favoured are those that make up the driver's name. A Mr Singh paid over £100,000 to buy MR51NGH in 2006, no doubt keen to keep up with his brother who had already bought S1NGH for £86,000 some years earlier. But there are some limits: plates that would make what the licensing authorities consider to be rude words are not allowed.

> **The first letter tells you where the car was first registered**

INDEX

ACKNOWLEDGEMENTS

Thanks to all the people who suggested objects that they felt should be included in this book, especially the British expats who listed the things they missed most from home and the many immigrants, temporary and permanent, who pointed out the oddities that had baffled, amused or interested them most when they moved to live in Britain.

Thanks too to CJ and Helen from the Design LAB at Manchester School of Art for their encouragement in developing this project.

We are also grateful to the organisations listed below for their help in the production of this book:

Food and Drink
Bitter & Twisted beer: Harviestoun Brewery. Brown sauce: Wilkin & Sons Ltd. Cadbury Creme Egg: Kraft Foods. English mustard: Unilever UK Ltd. Golden Syrup: Tate & Lyle Sugars. Irn-Bru: A. G. Barr plc. Kendal mint cake: George Romney Ltd. Marmite: Unilever UK Ltd. Orange marmalade: Wilkin & Sons Ltd. Polo mint: the 'Polo' name and image is reproduced with the kind permission of Societé des Produits Nestlé S.A. Scotch whisky: image of Old Pulteney 21-year-old courtesy of Inver House Distillers Ltd and Burt Greener Communications. Stinking Bishop cheese: Charles Martell & Son Ltd. Worcestershire sauce: the Lea & Perrins Worcestershire sauce name and image is reproduced with the kind permission of H. J. Heinz Ltd. Laverbread: supplied by The Fish Society. Pork pie: Pork Pie Appreciation Society (www. porkpieclub.com).

Clothing
Barbour jacket: Beaufort jacket courtesy of J. Barbour & Sons Ltd. Doc Martens boot: Airwair International Ltd. Fulton umbrella: A. Fulton Co. Ltd. Hunting pink: image of Grafton Hunt coat courtesy of Mears Country Jackets Ltd. Manchester United football shirt: Manchester United Ltd. Policeman's helmet: Greater Manchester Police. Royal Ascot Ladies' Day hat: Ilda Di Vico Couture Millinery (www.ascothats. net). School uniform: photo credit Stockport Grammar School, with thanks for permission to Mr and

Mrs Bassi and Rohan Bassi. 'Folk the Banks' T-shirt: Jamie Reid courtesy of Isis Gallery, UK. Wellington boot: Hunter Boot Ltd. Brogue shoe: Maxsol/shutterstock.

At Home
AGA cooker: AGA Rangemaster Ltd. Anglepoise light: Anglepoise Ltd. Dyson vacuum cleaner: Dyson. Hot-water bottle: quote from George Mikes taken from *How to Be a Brit*, André Deutsch 1984, permission courtesy of Penguin Books. Knife, fork and spoon: London cutlery by David Mellor Design Ltd. Teapots: (novelty) The Teapottery (www.teapottery.co.uk); (dotty) Emma Bridgewater. Royal Worcester wedding mug: Royal Worcester. Tesco carrier bag: Tesco plc.

Transport and Travel
A–Z street map: Geographers' A–Z Map Co. Ltd. Brompton bike: Brompton Bicycle Ltd. Eddie Stobart lorry: Eddie Stobart Ltd. Hackney carriage: copyright LTI Limited reproduced with permission; Fairway and TX shape is a registered design; FairwayTM, TXTM, the LTI device, the LTI, London Taxis International and The London Taxi Company logos are all trademarks of LTI Limited. JCB 3CX: J C Bamford Excavators Ltd. London Underground map: Transport for London. Mini: photo author DeFacto; file licensed under the Creative Commons Attribution-Share Alike 2.5 Generic licence. MINI: BMW UK Ltd. Morgan Three Wheeler: Morgan Motor Co. Ordnance Survey map: Ordnance Survey Ltd. Oyster card: Transport for London. Range Rover: Jaguar Land Rover Ltd. Red double-decker bus: Transport for London. Rolls-Royce Phantom: Rolls-Royce Motor Cars Ltd.

Sport and Leisure
Red nose: thanks to Comic Relief. Glamping tent: thanks to Tobyn Cleeves of Bell Tents (www.campingwithsoul.co.uk). Morris dancers' bells and hat: thanks to Duncan Broomhead and Adlington Morris Men. Pantomime dame's costume: dame played by Sam Oakes in Cheshire Youth Pantomime Society performance of *Snow White & the Seven Dwarfs*; photo by Helen Robinson, costume by Sonia Robinson, make-up by Kendal Tyne Love.

Out and About
Argos catalogue: Home Retail Group. Comic seaside postcard: images copyright of Bamforth & Co Ltd. Hille chair: Hille Educational Products Ltd. Mr Whippy ice cream van: Ian Super Whippy Ltd (www.MrWhippy.co.uk). Pub sign: Joseph Holt Ltd. Remembrance poppy: Royal British Legion.

THE AUTHORS

Geoff Hall is British. He is a graduate in Modern Languages from Oxford University, and holds a first-class degree in Three Dimensional Design and a Masters degree in Design from the Manchester School of Art. In addition to writing on design-related matters he teaches part-time on the Design course at Manchester.

Kamila Kasperowicz came to live in Britain from her native Poland three years ago and is ideally placed to recognise the peculiarities of British people and their everyday culture. She is a graphic designer, with a first-class degree from the University of Silesia. She has also completed a Masters degree in Design at the Manchester School of Art.

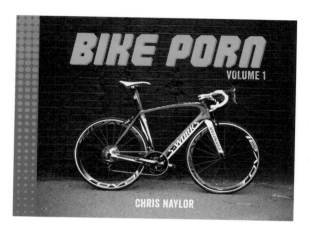

BIKE PORN

Chis Naylor

Hardback

978-1-84953-481-9

£14.99

**All bikes are beautiful,
but some are downright sexy.**

Bike Porn brings together stunning photographs of some of the most seductive and tantalising bikes ever made, from the slickest single-speeds to the most teched-out racing machines and beyond, captured in all their finely crafted glory.

If you're interested in finding out more about our books,
find us on Facebook at **Summersdale Publishers**
and follow us on Twitter at **@Summersdale**.

www.summersdale.com